The Pillowcase

by

M.T. Hardy

authorHOUSE®

AuthorHouse™ UK Ltd.
500 Avebury Boulevard
Central Milton Keynes, MK9 2BE
www.authorhouse.co.uk
Phone: 08001974150

First published by AuthorHouse 7/17/2008

ISBN: 978-1-4343-9233-6 (sc)

Printed in the United States of America
Bloomington, Indiana

This book is printed on acid-free paper.

Dedication

Written, with love and dedication, for Nicola, Rebecca, Abigail and dearest Oliver.

'Don't lose the wonder, of your eyes' (Van Morrison)

The Pillowcase

County Down -The North of Ireland, April 1979

As with so much else, it was the paradox that dominated. The mellowness of the Green fields harshly dissected by damp tarmac, winding unevenly amidst measured hedgerows and endless trees. Flecks of blossom competing with the Yellows and Browns of tired fields and buildings that kept livestock and secrets in equal measure. The scene was like few others and had no mirror to reflect what was hidden. Death was evident but only to those who knew.

The coded message and the map reference matched and two phone calls later the command was placed and so a silent ritual commenced. At 6.27am, Four Army Land Rovers moved within a mile of the site, each taking a position notionally linked to the points of the compass. Three minutes later, each unit began snaking their way on foot to an agreed point, the only noise permitted was that of feet and screaming hearts, such was the fear not admitted. Trip wires were sought along with evidence of disturbance in an otherwise untouched part of the countryside, unlikely to receive day-trippers or school parties. A radio conveyed the location of the units all correctly in place and at 7.33am, each soldier stopped and having engaged the cover command watched with eyes that did not blink. What they saw unfold before them was a procedure many had only witnessed on exercise. The simulation did not feel like this, thought one teenager, already so tense he could barely breathe. A Saracen stopped on the road, out of which emerged two individuals, awkward in movement inhibited by their suits but clear in intent, opening a rear door and lowering what looked like a child's toy pram. Watched by the unseen and with minimal delay, the remote controlled scanner moved smoothly for a handful of meters and stopped. An arm extended, with a spasm, from which a camera became evident. The image relayed to the monitor confirmed a picture that was expected and so offered a perverse comfort that there was no surprise. A hooded body, presumed male, wearing the uniform of Her Majesty filled a flickering screen that only that week had introduced colour. Hands were tied and the feet were without any footwear, socks or otherwise. A bleached white pillowcase concealed the simple truth of a bullet wound to the rear of the head, biased towards the left ear. Additional searching by the unloved robot indicated no other signs of secondary traps and so, with a lightness of tread that belied his size, the Officer approached the crumpled mass. He bent down and seemed to place a kiss on the cheek of the body but in fact was the rudimentary evaluation of life or death. The inspection of the corpse and issued information via radio merely stated the obvious. The name, that of Simon Jacks, a Corporal, was confirmed Seventeen minutes later at which point the stiffen remains were removed.

A military press release issued a few hours later drew a line under a familiar scenario, confirming that the IRA had claimed responsibility for the death of an occupying enemy agent. It went on to detail that the family were provisionally informed and told they would be visited by a Junior Officer within 48 hours, the purpose of which was to confirm that Simon Jacks was a loyal soldier, highly regarded, brave and a credit to his

Regiment. He could expect to be buried with honour with his colour party made up of his immediate comrades who would be granted special leave to travel back to the main land. The Army would meet the full cost of all funeral expenses although as a matter of policy would retain all items of his personal effects.

His parents were never told of the circumstances of their son's death other than it involved working on matters of great secrecy. Mrs. Jacks never really understood what that meant.

Chapter 1

Autumn 1996

The tedium of the drive wasn't helped by relentless drizzle that a poorly adjusted wiper only partially cleared. Sunday traffic had increased threefold in the thirty-six months of an unwelcome but necessary routine balancing work and home that co-existed some 133 miles apart. The opportunity to think, to reflect on what was being left behind was one of the few trades offs from the tedium. The thought processes always seemed to follow the same pattern. The beckoning quietness of a rented flat held both joy and foreboding. The rationalizing of the guilt in leaving behind the central if diminishing tenets of a disjointed life is quietly supplanted by the piecing together of the coming week. The river was barely visible on his left as he approached the 'Old High Street', that was neither old nor high. Right at the lights, second left, right again and the joy of parking. An evening of three papers and lightweight TV beckoned, again. Entry into the modern if chilled rooms never generated anything other than indifference. Phone messages, Three, were wiped unheard, for no apparent reason other than feeling they were unimportant to start with. Calls to his place of work and home were clipped and lacked feeling. They were calls of utility, stating he had arrived and was, seemingly, well. The quiet adjustment of creating a different type of order began. Seven shirts were placed alongside four suits, hung inside a wardrobe that was empty save for a pair of running shoes. Smaller items were neatly placed alongside each other, with a toiletry bag, bought as a twenty-first birthday present, placed precariously in the shower. Milk and other provisions were placed in a fridge that was otherwise redundant. The wardrobe, fridge and a shower that were bone dry, reflecting and symbolizing his absence.

Sports pages first, smiling wryly at the contradictions of pundits. Less analysis, more understanding he thought. Political comment next, failing to be taken in by the 'passion of policy'. Blair will be the chosen one, next year and who could argue that he wouldn't be an improvement on the current crowd. The Election next year made his mind switched immediately to 1979 and the bitterness he shared with Mr.Callenghan. 1979, a year to make the devil weep, he thought. Editorials were glanced at; money and business pages followed the same path as the phone messages with the magazines neatly stacked for the coming five nights. A feature on the shadow Home Secretary was read with puzzlement, being impressed with his enthusiasm for justice. Rare, in these modern times. The news was glanced at without sound, only to be introduced when Bath flashed a try against Wasps. A supper of Tuna and French bread, a shower and a deep sleep followed.

Neil Pearson had a notional regard for order. Quietness was preferred and enjoyed but silence feared. His predictability was born out of routine rather than obsessivness. In his external world he didn't like to assume or to judge and was at ease with his own intuition when making choices. He got on with things in a manner that was viewed as measured and without clutter. A kettle, a plate, a single cup, a narrow bed reflected this, allowing the world to shrink a little. The irrelevant excesses of goods and chattels are to be found elsewhere in the other place called home. He was relaxed with the perception that he lacked speed of thought or was dynamic. He preferred to be understood as thorough, a characteristic he knew irritated others. The internal domain that contained his other world was an altogether more complex structure of secrets, memories and buried feelings of intense and structural guilt. Still it continued, like the humming of a dimmer switch. Unhappiness and calm wrestled for the required space in his thinking. Calmness dominated presently. The setting of the alarm-6am- would introduce the commencement of Five, Thirteen hour's days in which success would be measured in the retention of the status quo. No change was good.

The flat plains of the vale revealed endless plastic canopies and the industries that were horticultural. The short drive through open countryside illustrated its blandness more so than when on foot although the flatness lacked the depth of Suffolk. A village, a single-track lane, turns right, then left and the stomach tightens. The lights pervaded the skyline in the late dawn, like a child's bedroom lamp in a darkened house. Every time he sees them he thinks of the etched unnaturalness of the Berlin wall, a wall that was also designed to keep people in. The lights did more than illuminate. They exposed, every night, the embodiment of original sin. 'Darkness is retained here, so dark it shines'; he recalled the words of a visiting priest. The flowerbeds added little to the view that this was a place that was unnatural. As a prison, it was not ordinary but Her Majesty welcomed you nonetheless. One Hundred stantions symmetrically place inside the perimeter, a Thousand lamps; enough for two airports ensnared by a wall as thick as a railway carriage and higher than his Third floor flat. The inner compound, landscaped by an Eighteen-foot steel slatted fence trimmed with razor wire and anti-helicopter landing grids, remained hidden. 'Colin' the German shepherd managed to get to 13 feet using teeth and paws, the record. No human 'Colin' had got half that height on the inner fence that seemed to become less visible the nearer you got. The cost to repaint the mesh a softer colour Green rather than the more oppressive Grey had been approved. The prisoners, four of them, had their complaint upheld by a thoughtful Chair of the Board of Visitors. Little did he know that it was to be funded from the Education budget, the Governor taking great joy in signing the virement. 'Less books it is then'. Victories were felt to be important. The camera's, the dogs, the pressure pads and human vigilance served to invite the observation that no one wanted to be here. Even the smell appeared to be watched. One road in, one entrance to and exit from a world of unimaginable tension and bleakness. A parody of Mr. Pearson's life perhaps. Not today. Today, he felt calm. The slow jog from the car to avoid more drizzle took him into the noisy void that was the staff shift change. Next week's detail being swapped, social lives being adjusted, fishing trips, golf matches and crib all being arranged at the expense of the state. This and the endless excess hours being fraudulently claimed. Goffman's statement that all institutions are run for the benefit of its staff seemed accurate. A joke, comments, views and opinions all merged into one crackle of noise. Twelve hours later will see the dialogue change again.

'Make way for a non-uniform man with backache: all that bowing and scraping, sir?' The comment was made in good humour and was received with equanimity. A grin quietly fixed on Pearson's face as he received his keys, radio and pager. He turned with a planned response,

'Wrong. The backache is caused by the number of complaints I've received from your wing, Mr.McBride.'

Along with the choked laughter and cries of mock derision, a suppressed comment was almost lost that made reference to another one being on its way. Probably about the standard of fire proofing on the curtains breaching some EU ruling. These were mostly good men and women doing a job that had little interest or value. And yet the skills needed to survive in such a world were undefined. The poor ones amongst them were known and displayed the delinquent traits of their charges.

The lightness of the encounter reflected the ease in which he moved amongst subordinates. The relationship was based on the virtues of honesty and directness, being part of but not one of them. It was also based on an open secret of an episode, not heroic, that enhanced his reputation with peers and junior colleagues but in eight short minutes, effectively ended any future career progression. He would do the same again, every time. Liked and respected but was too distant and private to engender the more extreme emotions of love and hate. A person also to whom the prisoners could talk and on occasions, confide. He always did what he said he would do but never make unconditional promises. He had never lied to a prisoner or their families or records anything on a file he wasn't prepared to explain, no matter how bleak or threatening. He loathed the pervasive secrecy of closed institutions and the manner in which information and stories would be stored and then used inappropriately or without recourse to their legal authenticity. Equally, he despaired at the conduct of his senior colleagues who shielded behind rules and protocols, endless standing orders or directives, as a means to get through the day. He routinely observed prisoners being lied to. He merely operated within his own self-defined creed of honesty. Never easy to justify some of the time but he recalled a friend from a previous life who would use the refrain 'if all else fails, try honesty'. Such was his style and presence of delivery, direct and without malice, each person he encountered knew his words were beyond reproach or challenge. When conveying points of detail, he was never wrong; such was his preparation and thoroughness. When release dates were confirmed for a life sentence prisoner or an appeal application turned down, he had experienced the human condition at its outer limits of joy and relief with that of sadness giving way to fear. It was not uncommon for prisoners to weep in his presence and no fewer than four had soiled themselves when being given a piece of news or information, that would condemn them further to time being spent in a the place deemed to denote a full-stop to one's life.

He found himself drifting towards his office, quietly reading a hand-written note from a staff member apologising for being late for some trivial training event last week. He had, by all accounts assisted at the scene of a Road traffic accident in which a child and its mother had been killed. Pearson was genuinely touched that this young staff member had retained a simple sense of courtesy to tell him what had happened and at the same time revealed more about his nature than a training event on 'Control and Restraint' ever could. He would contact him later. The room that doubled as a sanctuary for Senior Prison Staff seeking to avoid contact with anyone, having no phone, also enabled Pearson to shift heaps of paper in the manner of a post office clerk stamping letters. He sat quietly for a moment; deep into his chair which when slightly reclined enabled a view of some distant hills to at least offer the reassurance of something better outside. A glance at his watch compounded his tired irritation that the daily briefing was but Three minutes away. Why is it, he thought, that the things you enjoy doing least always seem to dominate.

The 'Morning Glory' as the meeting became known was something of a ritual designed to reinforce the image of those who attended at the exclusion of those who didn't. It was a mixture of gossip, rumour, supposition and general opinion exercised within the construct of a decision-making forum. Specific commands and standing orders were woven into un-minuted agreements that served to enforce acts of retribution. Power was wielded, a more arbitrary, benign form of that of the guard of the Third Reich allowing the movement or otherwise of Jews from Warsaw in the early days of the occupation but the net effect was not dissimilar. Staff careers were ended or launched, prisoner moves or special visits vetoed or approved depending less on the weight of argument than on the less than liberal doctrines of expediency or the omnipotent spite and revenge. Mood accounted for much. A bowel cancer operation was recently blocked on the basis that the prisoner had failed to co-operate with an internal investigation into a prison officer being implicated in drug smuggling. The official reasons given were medical and neatly illustrated the extent to which how the process of management could become so distorted. The concept of deserving causes was more in evidence than reasonableness.

Five Prison Governor Grades were in attendance, the senior managers of this modest but highly political provision known as'dispersal'. This odd phrase has Lord Mountbatten to thank for its introduction, being responsible for a report that recommended all of societies worst, most violent and criminally devious prisoners should be located or 'dispersed' within Nine establishments throughout the UK. All should be of maximum-security status and be run with an increased staff ratio. Two facilities should be designated as suitable to house prisoners with terrorist convictions and if their security risk was assessed as being so high, they are detained within a self contained secure unit. This policy replaced that of using the oxymoronic Isle of White as the principle receptacle of citizens who found normal living and behaviour beyond them, and making the humane treatment of mostly infamous prisoners somewhat easier. That, at least was the philosophy. The number One, the high priest, the man in whom everyone placed faith, Lionel Millet, chaired the meeting. He enjoyed being called Sir. He was Welsh, inconsistent, vindictive and a drinker, a man of many years' service seemingly set upon an Old Testament crusade against anyone with whom he did not approve. He was concerned less about the sinister behaviour of staff or the repressed awfulness of the conduct of prisoners than with the virtue of clean fingernails or polished shoes. He liked shirts to be ironed and women, as an accomplice but not as peers. He was not modern. His considerable personal authority and strength was founded upon creating the reality of control and security. The establishment reflected his style: ordered, lacking vision or drive but was administered within the tight parameters that staff enjoyed. 'Uniforms' liked him and his immediate peers, all much younger, regressed in his presence as a classmate would in the company of the bully. The exception was Pearson, who neither engendered the opportunity to be bullied or who felt the need for approval. His career could not be progressed by Millet and such was their relationship that it was unlikely to be ended either.

Functional heads were seated-Residential, Operations, Regimes, Estate and Security. The prison's deputy would appear occasionally when her ill health permitted. The Doctor never did. It lasted one hour and ended at exactly 8.45am. Coffee was served but never Tea, only Millet was allowed to smoke. The business was conducted in monologues and previously arranged ploys and signals that Pearson couldn't always read. The process worked and endured. Millet opened each session with the mantra- 'no escapes yesterday for which the public thanks you'. He would smile, unevenly, revealing perfect teeth set under thin lips of different shades of Red. A resume followed of the previous day's events and episodes with a short verbal report expected- 'Facts please, ideas tomorrow'. Residential always started, Security, the longest slot always concluded. Prison fabric, food, fish tanks, colour schemes, relocating a door from the library, refurbishment of the showers in the gym- it could have been a planning meeting for a new housing estate, Pearson thought. If only the public, who thanked us daily, really knew.

The cessation of prisoners work in the 'Plug Shed' and its closure for the next Five days was explained with the unconvincing air of authority that was based upon guess work rather than knowledge or clarity. Its closure-enabled dozens of prisoners to spend time inactive often used to plot and scheme and to tell stories. And lies. Millet feared inactivity the most and began to listen intensely on the reasoning. He was passive which did little to put Residential, a thin young man perspiring to the point of indicting a thyroid problem, at ease. Operation's makes the point that another day of prisoners in their cells wanking will cause an even bigger problem for the visiting optician. Pearson winced, expecting better from a colleague eight years his junior but with a considerable intellect. She looked startled having made her joke and was relieved to note Sir laughed, in three short bursts of equal duration. 'Resolve this problem today please', was the edict that went unheard at Residentials' peril. Her other comments, about the introduction of prisoner treatment plans and the outline staffing levels of the new sex offender block, located on Echo wing were measured and thoughtful. Their articulation and the manner in which they were presented was more in keeping with this intense character who personified the nearest thing to a friend Pearson had at work. More consultation was needed, she concluded.

Further comments rumbled around until Millet fixed Pearson with a familiar gaze. Liking each other or otherwise was never acknowledged. They had worked with each other at two previous establishments, separated by Nine years during which time both had grown apart. Millet had aged and experienced the trauma of watching his wife quietly fade with some awful terminal illness had compounded his resentment towards others, especially prisoners. His need to control and with it, the desire to exercise authority irrespective of the purpose was now a feature of every discussion. Humour or banality had long since moved out being replaced by dourness and an odd personal odour that others thought was a mask for his excessive drinking. Pearson in a different form of contrast had become quiet, more introspective and highly wary of colleagues or at least those who were his immediate peers whom he regarded as people who placed themselves at the centre of their work.

He would prefer a greater bias towards prisoners and the belief that they too were important. Their immediate differences, that once stimulated debate and argument was now put to one side. The task was everything. Yet Millett's position was unchallenged and even Pearson knew his limitations, choosing to avoid any prolonged confrontation.

'Security; about whom or what are you displeased today? Any tunnels found'?

The mocking tone in his voice was his honest attempt at sarcasm but its delivery indicated that malice was absent. Pearson located his notes and as is always the case, others listened. The importance Millett placed on his words was evident, including those unspoken. He displayed a different form of attentiveness, more solemn, less accusing. In moments of rare personal acknowledgment, he commented in incomplete sentences that Pearson was his eyes, his ears and his barometer. Millet wanted his look, his calmness, the faded but evident fitness, regretting the mess lunches and routine consumptions of cheap Vodka that had taken its toll. A tension always existed when the leader had less bearing than the subordinate and it was apparent again this morning.

'Eleven security reports have been received over the weekend which incidentally was very quiet. Four were anonymous, presumed from prisoners, given the forms used. The other's detailed various accounts of dealing and brewing; the association of Hassan and Khan was again commented upon with a specific reference to the level of intimidation being applied- this is the fourth report in Ten days. The most worrying was an overheard remark made by an officer to Tressler, the South African on Delta about changing fifty pence's'.

The prison could ill afford another corruption scandal involving officers selling fifty pence pieces for double their value so enabling some prisoners to hold large sums of cash in a market place where notes were forbidden and the personal allowances highly regulated. As with life elsewhere, more money meant the ability to influence and so control.

'Name of the officer' Millet snapped.

Pearson declined to offer it, despite it being written in front of him, until he had completed his own investigation into what might prove to be an innocent remark. Once Millett was aware of the name, at the very least that officer would constantly find his career in a cul-de-sac, irrespective of the circumstances. Pearson was keen to avoid the doctrine of no smoke without fire and so indicated he needed to check which officer to whom the alleged remark was made as two colleagues shared the same surname.

'The four unsigned reports all related to Collingsworth needing to be removed or he would be marked'.

He placed the emphasis on this euphemism for a simple but very deep cut, neatly administered using a craft knife, usually starting from just in front of the left ear and finishing in the lower right jaw. The cut would be deeper and longer if he was held. Pearson fleetingly visualised an inmate who had his phallus removed and placed in the extended cavity of his mouth that had been increased by several inches. The scribbled note deposited on that occassion on the cell door read; "he said that the only time he smiled was when he had a cock in his mouth, so he's happy now". The prisoner bleed to death although the names of the culprits were easily located given they were placed on fifty nine separate reports such was the level of disapproval. He continued, providing a short but specific analysis of what the responses were to be and when. He gained no pleasure in allowing injury or drunkenness or the unchecked corruption of an officer seeking to clear some credit card debt. Everyday chaos of prison life or just life, he reflected. Prison was a place in which people were secure but never safe. Or at least that was how it seemed.

He was never interrupted and answered questions with an unhurried simplicity often associated with personal authority.

'The significance of Hassan's and Khans association'? Millett was concentrating hard as he opened questions.

'Given Hassan's contacts, it would appear he is trying to use Khan's outlets to recommence dealing whilst here. I've had one substantive phone discussion with the Met. They have confirmed a series of observations that has linked associates of both men. One phone taped recording was described as "unhealthy" which I thought was quaint'. A smile flickered on Millett's face but he said nothing. Pearson concluded.

'All the data being supplied by the police are pointing a finger at these Two who will use their position here to exploit outlets. There is every likelihood that the pair of them virtually controls all the stuff coming in here also. Khan's visitors are now stripped searched and the visit is filmed. Hassan rarely receives visits so we suspect his kit is being brought in by any number of contacts, daily.'

Those present knew the next part of the process; an activity guaranteed to increase prison tension but was never avoided. One of these pair, Khan, would be 'ghosted' out of the establishment, never again being given the official opportunity to mix with his business associate. Ghosting was a form of hidden internment. It involved the removal of a prisoner from their cell, usually in the very early hours of the morning, placed in isolated segregation for a few hours and then transported to a place of comparable security status. Options by definition were limited. The prisoner is not consulted or pre-warned or given any right of appeal. The application of Body constraints is the norm. Families are advised after the move is completed. Pearson often wished the ghosting effect could be applied to staff.

'I think we can agree that one of these pair, Khan, be move.'

Millett invoked his authority as a glance was flashed between estates and regimes who wondered why it could not be the more disruptive Hassan. They of course were not privy to Pearson's file that stated that Hassan should under no circumstances be transferred without ministerial approval. And who could be bothered to get that. Iraqi's generated much interest. The notes would record that after considerable thought and careful consideration of the options, the relevant standing order would be applied to maintain good order and discipline- a catch all phrase that could be used to justify anything. Pearson was required to take care of these arrangements and was already way ahead of his colleagues. He would be careful to appraise the Principle Security Officer with a high degree of precision and make the point for officers detailed to carry out the exercise to be well prepared. Door stepping a cell required more than bravado. Khan could be very volatile, thus Six Officers would be deployed. 'No socks', Pearson directed, a reference to the habit some officers had of forcing such garments into the mouths of prisoners as a matter of routine. Or sport, almost. Once removed, Pearson would place some calls with his counterparts to horse trade. One-for-one, always predicated on favours. The police would be alerted given Khan's category A status, to agree a transport route. Once these arrangements were in place, the order could be issued and so giving Khan's prison career another if un-welcomed twist. Removing him would create the pleasing illusion of exercising authority but little else. Power remained with the inmates. The unspoken aspects of this decision were also present in the room. They remained so as all members of prison staff were aware that the grasp they had on control was tenuous. The removal of such a high profile prisoner would create an un-welcomed tension that could result in a death, a suicide or a sustained period of unrest- the type which saw Millett at his worst; absent. They were all hoping that tomorrow had been and gone, the task completed. Personal fear was never publicly acknowledged.

This prison, unlike virtually all others, concentrated the wider public's cast offs within its walls. They have decreed that some of its number had forfeited the right to live within it. Some forever. Of the Three hundred and Seventy nine inmates on the official role, Two Hundred and Seventy Three had extinguished the life of another citizen. The methods varied from the planned to the mistakes, from the haphazard outbursts of rage to the indiscriminate episodes of mayhem. The net effect was identical. People dead, leaving behind the resented disruption to ordinary lives. And tears. Death is able to offer itself in so many different ways. The child left in the boot of a car, abandoned on a hillside in December, to be found frozen, holding herself as a mother would a pillow after childbirth. This, the consequence of a kidnap in which the bounty was paid but the prize never given. The location of the car was incorrectly recorded, resulting in the search being carried out in the wrong place. The man, who did this, mixes with contract killers, the bombers, the sadist's, the wronged husband's and those who claim their innocence. This mixture was enriched by the quiet presence of others who are the natural predators of those who do not speak for themselves and who view adult males as people who are safe and strong; children, always children, the elderly with their stories, women whom they rape. Friends, leaders, organisers, helpers and potential partners one minute, brutal assailant the next. The heady mix of power and pleasure. And what of the Armed Robber's? No axe to grind, do your time and get on with it. Just guns to point and corn to harvest. They are the noise and conscious of the prison, the arbiters of reasonableness. They allow the man who has abused countless children to serve tea to a Sikh extremist who, in the pursuit of defending the Punjab, shot a sub-postmaster. This political assassination was ordered as the deceased was importing high quality Heroin through his video outlet. Robbers, always talking, pleading, calming, trading, referring. The taking of the extra visiting orders was a small hardship to bare but worth it. For the staff at least. Like no other institution, darkness was present in every crevasse as behaviour from outside was neatly dovetailed into the inside. For the place to run, the exercise needed to be premised on surprise, vindictiveness and collusion. Guess work and often bogus intelligence helped rationalise difficulties, not always the preserve of the Governor. The prisoners, virtually but not all, had transcended reasonableness and what the psychologists call 'personal control' hence their incarceration. And yet their lives simply continued unseen but not different.

The prison was a community and arranged itself with a deftness that Town Planners would envy. Desirable landings, or otherwise created a living monopoly board in which each individual knew their domain. District's, along with the prison equivalent of pubs, corner shops, eating venues, betting offices and at least three hairdressers all provided a much needed service, despite being forbidden. A rule ignored. Different smells would denote the resident's quarter and how they lived their lives. Robbers; casual, immaculate for visits, after-shaved and groomed. Sex Offenders with the pallid presence of sweat brought on by the anxiety of always watching and never going out for exercise. Sikh's and Muslim's, their lives governed by the next meal and prayer, create part of the sub-continent with a subtle mix of simple cooking spices and constant talking but no listening. Bookish, quiet domestic murderer's form clubs organise collections and form important relationships with prison visitors. They also do some fetching and carrying of packages, the contents of which are never disclosed, just delivered. And the terrorist's, a brotherhood apart, who mix and discuss in an atmosphere one associates with a queue at a soccer match. Furtive whispers with rowdy laughter but always dialogue: the least dependent, unproblematic of all inmates. Yet guilty of the greatest collective grief.

The jail opens, for its inhabitants at least, at 6.30am. Five key strokes in the central control room triggers the 'clicks', as each cell on each landing on each wing opens electronically. Prisoners will begin to emerge and go about their routines.

To collect breakfast, papers and to exchange tea and favours, cigarettes and yesterday's Times and to collect winnings and pay debts. Some offer prayer's, many stretch and a few will descend deeper into a tunnel that has no light. Dates and day's are everything. Each new one brings with it a resonance of an anniversary. Birthdays, weddings, deaths, trials, appeals, tariff's, exam or blood test results. It might be a day for a visit, or not. Or to remember the Munich Air crash. Relentlessly, each day is representative of no change, no difference from last year and yet everything moves on. For one prisoner, the day is remembered for the receipt of the Royal prerogative of mercy, having been sentenced to be hanged almost forty years previously. The Wandsworth hanging chamber had already completed Twenty Three trials, simply to ensure no problems were encountered on the day. The reprieve was exercised Seventy Two Hours and the prisoner has lived ever since. Twenty Seven years at this lodging, being moved in on the opening day. To look at him now is to beg the question of whether the young Elizabeth and her privy counselors were wise. He cried with disappointment when the news came through, so the rumour goes. It is unlikely that his child victims shed similar tears, other than of fear before they were quietly suffocated. He now enjoys the status of being identified as 'that's him' resonating like some Slavic surname and corresponds worldwide with collectors of stamps. Real marriages end and phantom ones begin. Relationships develop and evolve as they might anywhere. Togetherness and partnerships matter to humans and small details like gender are not spoken about or overlooked. Contact is pursued, dates are arranged and with it the excitement of a sexual encounter is generated. Hands are held, necks stroked and the learning of how to fit within each other's space is worked on. Cards and notes are exchanged, special signs and knowing greetings are acknowledged out of which arises a new togetherness. It does more than pass the time. Ultimately, the relationship is consummated, either emotionally or physically, by whatever method is tolerated. For this is how ordinarily heterosexual men are able to survive in a world without a female partner. Becoming gay or embracing the state of existence that is homosexual is not countenanced. That in the main is still the preserve of others, of whom the majority disapprove. They simple change the perception of gender. Adaptability being one of the characteristics of humans that allow for advantage over less developed forms of mammals. Such relationships endure to the point of transfer or release or the diminishing of feeling that can never be explained anywhere. One moment, a passion that can have no greater depth. The next, an indifference matched with a sneer or dismissed with a glance. Or even death. Thereafter, the quiet moments of intimacy, the expressions of hope, desire, of shared needs are denied and suppressed. Maleness then resurfaces and with it the conventions which deny that pleasure and certainty can be achieved from anywhere. And the joy and guilt which transient sexual encounter's can bring. For one inmate, answerable to the name only of 'lips', a neat business has been sustained that enables him, as one convicted of the murder of a twelve year old, to survive. He has removed virtually all his teeth in order to sell the service of fellatio to those who either wish it or to watch, the later being cheaper. They drink, play cards, 'screw', gamble, read, discuss Marx , write, think, cook, share, lend, fight, wound, paint , destroy, love, build and lie. They always lie. Like any community, nothing is what it seems. And still the Robbers talk.

Breakfast, a choice of Three options, make's way for a mixture of work, education classes, special visits or queuing for medicines. The prison was at its best, most relaxed in the mornings. The expectations that an afternoon visit yields, especially, creates a mellow sense of joy. Letters arrive at 10'O'clock, designed to be available for those returning to the wing some Two hours later, to be opened with relish or fear. Letters, the mid-day meal, four choices, and the pre-visit shower. Best jeans and ironed sweat shirt, borrowed scent. All to impress 'my people'. The contents of often ill written A4 and the words exchanged in a crowded meeting hall will determine the mood of the rest of the day. Either medium, written or in person, will express the need for forgiveness but lost appeals, death, illness or the more mundane explanation about a lost letter or a missing National Geographer. All will add to or detract from the tension. Missed visitors or worst of all delayed escorts for Category A citizens will create unimaginable rage that will get displaced within minutes. Visits which conclude with 'so this is it...'and the rage clock begins to tick. Most assaults and serious incidents occur during the Tea period, around 4.30pm, suicides attempts an hour or so later. 'Bang up', at 9pm will clamp down any number of stories of hopelessness and fear. As the lights shut down, the image of row's of terrace houses , too, closing for the night, hiding different pre-occupations but not dissimilar. To think a single letter, its content unexpected can create such a loss of control that Three weeks ago, a prisoner was hit with a hammer whilst sitting watching the News. The way Anglo Saxon's organise their society and form rules was exemplified in this prison. Everything and nothing was here.

As the meeting concluded, with it the huddled ritual of whispered comments, operations caught Pearson's eye, mouthing the need to 'have a word'. Ruth Mills was, in Pearson's eyes, the acceptable face of the prison service. Hugely bright but self deprecating, sharp witted and very able to strong arm officers Twenty years her senior. She presented as someone who was fun to be with until an unhappiness set in that pushed colleagues and friends away, to be replaced by a vacuum in which sadness lived. Her clipped, ordered demeanour would give way to a look of uncertainty and indifference. Her face could change by the minute. Pearson, in a rare moment of unguarded personal charity once described her as 'handsome'. He later qualified the comment as to mean good looking without the encumbrance of being pretty, well dressed without being striking or simply glamorous. He meant it as an unconditional compliment. She took it as the ultimate Red-Light in female attractiveness. To be described as handsome at Thirty Six was not cool or good news, especially from a colleague who's opinion on just about everything else, she rated. Had anyone else offered the view then perhaps the Northern temper might twitch a little. Oddly, she knew what he meant; she just wished he wasn't so accurate.

They weren't in any real sense close either as friends or mates given their time spent in the past few years was grounded in work. They started on the same day, she on a promotion, him on a transfer shrouded in rumour. Good colleagues, who would share the occasional sandwich and bleat about the system. Her more than him. Paperwork, lack of scope, the outrageous colour of pink on E wing. They would talk about work in the abstract, politics would also warrant a mention and given her previous life as an investment broker, PEPS. They were relaxed in each other's company as only non-lovers could be. Their respective ages allowed a layer of conversation to be missed out. Personal reflections were just that. Comments about style or an approach to an issue was not some heavy handed or coded form of flirting. Or criticism; an aspect in which personal power was being exploited. They were equals in every sense, with Ruth feeling at ease in his presence and safe. He, likewise admiring her ability to enlighten a room of dull men with an innocent reference to the length of skirts some visitors wear. As with all relationships that work, it's what was not spoken about that defines its quality and ability to endure. Home-life, reference to personal time and interests, partners, previous jobs, cars, holidays and the many other things which define character were absent from their dialogue. Neither felt the need to ask. Pearson was aware that she lived with a Merchant Banker in a home described by an officer as bigger than Old Trafford but little else. She knew his daughter,

Emma, was about to start University, that he was married, lived miles away and went running most mornings. This absence of information was felt unimportant, so was never discussed. Why should it, as it served no purpose.

'Why Khan?'

'Hassan has a no-move embargo stamped on his card-Foreign Office thing.'

'He will create very loudly. This is his fourth ghosting in Nine months'.

'He needs to be moved for everyone sake. If you think differently, I'll delay things until tomorrow when we can discuss it with our leader. Your call.'

He seemed puzzled by her preoccupation for Khan- a man who removed the ears and seven fingers of a man who failed to pay a debt of £211. He sensed that there was more to be said and his eye caught her mood.

'Are you.. .' and before the OK could leave the voice box, she deftly switched into a different mode, dismissing the enquiry with a curt intonation, suggesting they discuss matters later.

Four short calls to his team and Khan's fate was neatly packaged. With that task complete he could prepare himself for an excursion to the wings. This was his natural domain and an environment in which he felt totally at home.

Chapter 2.

The route to the main body of the Prison required the passing through of four gates, electronically opened with each step closely watched on a bank of seventeen monitors located in the control room. This room, off limit's to all bar a few was part of Pearsons domain. Ninety nine percent boredom, One percent critical. The voice box located at each gate would require a coded response in order to allow the movement to proceed unheeded. The arrival at the main entrance into the centre from which each wing flows requires a person to again identify themselves before two further doors are 'clicked'. One percent doubt and you don't open it, is Pearsons guidance: simple and effective, no matter who is inconvenienced. The reception area is a mixture of the utilitarian and Trust House Forte. Poor quality paintings hang along-side copied masterpieces. A fish tank in which a Human could swim is the preserve of one inmate who diligently cares for 'his firm'. A robber of course. Low-backed easy chairs, poorly watered plants and the smell of bleach pervades what is a busy thoroughfare. East meets west here, the place through which each prisoner will walk when going to a visit, a different wing, the kitchens, the gym, the chapel, the library or the 'canteen'. It was also the junction from which the occasional individual is released or carried if deceased. A notice board adorns the dominant wall as the doors open onto which messages are posted for inmates. The attempt at creating an atmosphere in adults can thrive is worked at, with staff realising that at any stage during the time when prisoners are unlocked, they are out-numbered five to one. Dynamic security was everything. The centre also provided access to the segregation unit, the 'seg': a prison within its own parameter's into which are placed those who are the most violent, the unstable, those who seek protection and those who need to be calmed. No one enters this unit unless escorted in and out. It is not without irony that Pearson finds it the calmest place in the jail and an arena in which staff show the hidden compassion that creates the air of civility. First name terms are encouraged, dialogue promoted and solutions worked at to reconcile problems. Only Two prisoners are unlocked at any-one time so minimising the potential for quiet acts of vengeance to be administered or scores being balanced. Twelve beds facilitated calmness.

Pearson's walk to the centre had an air of pursuit about it. Not hurried but representing a sense of focus and the manner of business that is to be done here. Once, when bored, he worked out that on one weekend duty, he walked Four Miles. Suicides do create work. As the gate unlocked, Pearson was greeted several times by different individuals, many with no axe to grind, inmates out of politeness. He always acknowledged this simple convention as though it was truly meant. The purpose of his arrival was to take the morning's applications: a prison ploy that fosters dependency and is actually unnecessary, he felt. That discussion could be saved for Ruth. The application process enabled prisoners access to a senior Governor upon whom demands could be placed and questions asked; a sort of ward round for the criminal world. Batches of papers were left at the required place into which he delved to find a modest four requests. Two on Alpha wing, one on Delta, the other in the segregation unit, always carried out last.

'Good morning, Sir', a quiet greeting being offered by a small, senior officer named Jacob.

'I'm detailed to escort you this morning, on detached duty from Gartree'.

'Hello Jacob. I'll assume that you have had a basic run down of what is required, all fairly simple really. We can do Delta first, Alpha second.'

Handing his colleague the four applications he caught a glance of Ruth further along the walkway. He eased towards her and managed to get within earshot before she noticed.

'I'll try and make this next refrain sound original and sincere- is everything OK?'

Ruth stared at the space between his right eye and the start of his hair line, rather than the usual contact. The pause that lasted no more than a second indicated a degree of unsettlement not usually associated with her. It was her turn to delay what she intended to say, only to put in its place something altogether more banal.

'Much better now, thanks'.

Friends instinctively detect dissonance and it was present now but Pearson did not pursue and retreated back to Jacob, a man who seemed to be balanced and something of an authority on Dickens, using every opportunity to quote Hard Times or passages from Bleak House- the symbolism appearing a touch contrived to the recipient to these lengthy discourses. Entry on to Delta wing was delayed for some Ten minutes, following an unpleasant incident in which an inmate had been attacked, being hit with a battery in a sock. With order restored, Pearson and his personal Open University settled into the wing office, whilst a man named Mace was called for over the internal speaker system.

The application merely indicated a need to 'see Mr. Pearson, the governor grade who is responsible for matters of prison security'. The wing office was a mixture of boxes and furniture, orange and blue, positioned to accommodate dialogue if not promote it. Mace entered the room, gestured to shake hands with intended precipitants of his comments and sat down. His angular frame, located a space on the edge of a very low armchair, suggested unease but not hostility. He looked grey, with dull blue eyes, teeth which lacked hygiene and a sense of personal grooming that was absent. He commenced the discussion in an accent rooted on the fringes of London and one that had received a higher education. Teacher training college perhaps. Pearson looked at him passively and immediately recalled who and what Mace was about. This sifting included a clear grasp of the nature of the crime committed and length of sentence, including time already served. Jacob took a note although he had no knowledge of what was moving around his colleagues mind.

'Can I be direct with you, Mr Pearson?'

'You may Mr Mace', Pearson responded in an un-hurried manner and one that promoted calmness in the questioner.

'I remain of the view that my category status is being retained for purely vindictive reasons. It has no basis in law, legal or moral. For eleven years it has prevented my progression through an inwardly corrupt system and each time I am refused, I never ever receive an explanation. Do you have a view?'

The question was put with an emphasis one might place on whether you agree with the sentiments of Peter at the Last Supper. Pearson had watched Mace's reluctance to make eye contact and established a feel for the tension in his voice. Each related characteristic conveyed resignation given Mace already knew what to expect.

'I do have a view and I suspect you know what it is'.

Mace sat forward to the point that Jacob thought he was about to slip off the chair, such was the awkwardness of his frame. His body seemed to defy gravity.

'No I don't actually so please indulge me'.

Even though indulgence was on neither parties mind, Pearson saw this as a green light for directness. He was already bored with the contrived, superior tone given it was self evidently counter- productive. He preferred conversational dialogue in order to convey and receive information. Question and answer sessions were to be avoided and he sensed this was about to become one.

'The security status of any prisoner is based on the level of risk they would pose were they to escape. Equally, the level also takes into account the need for supervision of visits and contact with others. Each of these aspects have, I have no doubt been explained to you. Your status has been retained given you are perceived to still present a risk. The interruption was swift.

'By what criteria am I to be judged?'

'Three things are considered in the main. The nature of your original offences, the attitude displayed towards the victims or their families and aspects of your personal psychopathy and general level of insight. Serious consideration is given to your potential to escape. It's about the level of risk you pose.'

'Insight into what?'

'Your offences'

An uneasy pause checked the exchanges. Pearson led at this point.

'Eleven years is a long time but when you evaluate your response to your conviction then you can safely assume many more years are in front of you unless..'

The interruption was anticipated and so it came.

'Unless what?'

'Unless you realize that being perceived as dangerous and a risk to the wider community, both in prison or outside then your world will be one of escorts, everywhere. Set about doing some work on your attitudes and values towards women in particular and citizens in general and you might progress. But that particular journey starts by removing the pornography, the pictures, the books and work with those who can help you to start thinking differently. Psychologists, Probation Officers, wing staff. That work will conclude when you reconcile what you have done is wrong in a way that sets you apart from others. I could go on but as an intelligent man I hardly think I am saying anything original. Currently, you are perceived to be a serious and unpleasant risk and what is more, I've signed the authority to retain the status for the past Two years and will do so again until your address the points that have been made. Now, do you have a view?'

Jacob shuffled as he sensed Mace had stopped listening.

'My view is that this concept of dangerousness is flawed and arbitrary.'

'People who are recatorgorised have tended to take themselves more seriously than you Mr Mace. But I might be wrong of course'

'You are Mr. Pearson.'

He stretched and stood up and moved quietly to leave in a child like way, struggling with the door handle. Jacob intervened and assisted. Mace then enquired if the door should be left. It should be Pearson insisted.

As they moved between venues in which the next application was to be heard, Pearson gave Jacob a rudimentary outline of mace's offences. Outwardly, a man of quiet charm married and rooted in the village community with the interest and spirit to match-church, photography club, and rambler and employed by the local authority as benefits adviser to the disabled. Privately, a sadist who murdered two prostitutes implicated in a third and conspired to kill three others. The police investigation revealed a man with a disturbing history of two name and several address changes, the last of which housed a room of unimaginable squalor from which his wife was barred entry. Such was his control she did not question the reason or motive, assuming the best; a hobby room of sorts perhaps. It was in fact a place in which torture was administered. His only recorded comments on tape when questioned by the police amounted to little more than a dismissive swipe.

'Well, we all need a room in which we can play. Where else can I go if it's raining?'

He was detected having been identified by another, potential victim by chance when taking her mother to an advice centre. He became agitated and persistent when an argument ensued about a care attendant's allowance for her to look after her mother. She was overheard to say words to the effect of 'we all have secrets, especially at night so you either approve the claim or I'll tell.' A supervisor got involved, the exchanges became even more acrimonious and the police called. Mace was questioned along with the women who indicated that he was known regular of what passed for the red light district of the nearest provincial town. She actually implicated him in a suggestion that he wanted favours for allowing the claim, which in fact was a lie but enough to set the ball rolling. Eventually, the house was searched which revealed an altogether bigger secret. He was convicted with a very long recommendation, Twenty years, and has remained stuck ever since. He never speaks to prison staff, reads science fiction endlessly and refuses contact with anyone who seeks it.

'Dickens frequented prostitutes did he not?'

Jacob came alive and was quick to defend his mentor indicating that he only offered help and guidance.

'Victorian philanthropist? There was I thinking he was a writer'

The entry to Alpha wing was much calmer. A three way discussion between two officers and Pearson indicated that the next application could be very problematic. The prisoner, a man named Flowers was making a serious complaint of assault, having that morning been transferred from Charlie wing. An incident the previous day had not been fully documented or recorded and the two officers, Principal and Senior in grade presented at being anxious and uncertain about what had happened. They looked almost childlike in their respective uncertainties, keen to displace the tension that was evident. Pearson put both men at ease and enquired into what was the presenting difficulty. Jacob was asked to arrange an office and then sent to bring the prisoner but not before his calmness had been established. Pearson propped himself against a radiator and with a few minutes Flowers entered, limping, with his shirt heavily soiled with blood. His face had been lifted from a car crash but he was seemingly calm. The officers made the point that he had refused to wash, change or see a doctor until his application had been dealt with. He invited both officers to sit in on the interview that commenced with Pearson inviting a squat, rounded Yorkshireman, John, to provide an overview of what had been established. Sensing that Flowers retained an impassive demeanour, he indicated that the account should be as detailed as the circumstances required.

'It seems fairly evident to me sir that one of the officers on the three's landing lost it, late on yesterday. Flowers moved from Charlie at four o'clock as planned. Straightforward cell swap, all cleared, no problem. He was bedded and kitted by seven and settled. Ten minutes before bang up all was quiet and no one was anywhere they shouldn't be. Shut down came and went; lates have gone off, nights on, all logged. I'm on again at seven to find Flowers in this state . He's virtually out of it, not in his cell and a right mess. Eight teeth have gone, jaw, nose , left eye shut-well you can see but he totally refused to see anyone before you. He was happy to wait, even.'

Pearson, internally felt puzzled as to why he was not summoned first thing but felt to raise this point now would change the mood, negatively.

'All he would say was that it's one of ours and it happened when he had a bathroom run at about Five o'clock. The blood was still very fresh so it fits. I pressed him like hell to say who did it, what happened and all that. Nothing. The tension on here is very high and we're not use to it. Something isn't right. Control said he was unlocked at five zero six and his door was clicked Twelve minutes later but he wasn't in his cell.

'Who was on?'

'Not clear and it's a right bodge. The detail says one name, the log another, the key tally something different. Gerry's working on that now but its suspect.

'Perhaps I should talk with Mr Flowers now and form a judgement about whether or not this is a police matter.' It already was, Pearson new.

'Who is favourite?'

'Don't quote me, but Colin from Delta'

'Colin?'

'Colin Smart and I'll explain later'

Jacob too felt very unsettled with so much dialogue in front of an inmate. An indication of Pearson's style no doubt but was it necessary, he pondered.

They both sat down and asked if the prisoner was happy to talk and he was. He also agreed that he needed medical treatment which he would receive after his interview.

'Mr Flowers, it is evident that you have been badly assaulted. Neither of us need to waste time adopting positions of distorting what happened or trying to add on any sense of justification.'

Jacob had left the room and returned with a glass of water, for himself such was his stomach troubling him.

'I gather that you are alleging a member of the prison service assaulted you earlier this morning. Have I got that correct?'

'Yes'

'Do you have any idea who it was and why? Clearly there are elements of what happened that are of real concern not least of which are your injuries.'

Flowers spoke with a quiet, Scottish bias and was totally still in his chair. He was struggling to talk through the swelling; such was the size of both lips and the taughtness of his jaw.

'Firstly, because I'm gay I suspect.' Candid and direct, Pearson thought.

He proceeded to ask a whole series of questions, covering each aspect of the incident from the beginning or at least from the point Flowers had been let out of his cell. This process revealed that Flowers had, on three previous occasions, provided this officer with a specific sexual service. In return, the officer paid him Five pounds "in silver". The officer only worked nights and each party would make an arrangement to be around at a given time, when Flowers went to the bathroom. On each of the three previous occasions, the officer had been a passive recipient of "work". This time he requested Flowers do something that was painful and in fact, he suggested, he didn't like. The refusal was met with anger and the subsequent loss of control. The short summary was met with a simple ultimatum: he gets moved or I'll have him charged. He will make my life difficult. It's your choice. One that Pearson had made some minutes earlier, to match his judgement to involve the Police.

Pearson felt quietly beguiled by this mans dignity. No demands or some great expectation. Reason was present in all what he had spoken or implied. Five minutes of pleasure will result in a dismissal and a grudge. Human kind was living up to Pearson's expectations even if they did not match those of Flowers.

'Did he approach you?'

'No. I offered. It was evident he was seeking some form of attention as we has already had something of a discussion previously when I was on D wing. I saw the benefits that the extra money could buy. I also concede that it is a sordid world.'

Jacob sensed that he was in the company of someone feeling ill at ease within his own skin. The dialogue was muted but not without courtesy. He felt that Pearson's focussed was too biased towards that of the prisoner and yet at no stage did he feel able to comment. The determined yet unhurried nature of his approach did not allow for space in which others might inhabit.

Pearson left the inmate to the attention of the medics and spoke quietly to the senior officer. That afternoon, Smart was to be phoned, suspended and no doubt, sent to hell. Jacob was indignant, claiming to have heard it all now and was preoccupied with his sense of outrage. His Calvinism shone through although Pearson was envious of the fact that he could still be shocked. They moved on, keys twisting, their step becoming swifter. The concluding inmate visit was to take place, as already pre-ordained in the segregation block and curiously, a visit that was to return Pearson to a different kind of hell to that of Smarts and no less expected.

Chapter 3.

The entry to the segregation unit involved various controlled requests to the voice box and the agreed coded chatter. As they walked across the inner compound, the prevailing sense of order was apparent, as if some invisible dust had been sprinkled to generate the aura of the Scottish highlands. They walked at a brisk pace. Clearance was asked for and granted to enter the unit: a facility designed to isolate, repair and control.

'A man named Liam O'Dell has asked to see you', remarks made by a short, thin officer of West Country origin.

'I'm not familiar with that name. Any ideas?'

'Arrived four days ago on a lay down. Very unhappy, apparently. Moved on a ten-seventy order. Cat A , Irishmen , IRA. Will no doubt want to see you in order to apologise to his victims'.

Pearson glanced at Jacob to register his disapproval for such a remark but felt no great need to comment. He felt caught slightly unaware. All Catorgory A movements go across his desk, especially those with known with the initial profile of O'Dell. He was also puzzled that the name had not been mentioned at his earlier meeting. This was unlike Millet who was anything but forgetful. He again asked what he wanted, only this time of the duty officer.

'Nothing recorded other than a wish to speak with "the Prison Management".

Pine air freshener and garlic formed the dominant smell. This space had a calmness all of its own. The small office, neatly kept was next door to the small kitchen. A court exercise yard was placed in the centre of the eight cells that formed the basis of what housed the great unwanted or not tolerated. Tea was offered but declined as Pearson busily read the reception details on his next call. It revealed that he arrived four days ago, from Full Sutton prison, moved for security reasons. It stated that he became very preoccupied about home, constantly making comments about needing to get out. Refuses to discuss anything when approached and started to associate with a known escapee. A decision to move him was acted upon quickly. A file, of four pieces of paper all of differing colours provided an outline of Liam Thomas O'Dell, known and respected member of the provisional's. Life sentenced imposed in 1980, the bulk of which has been served in the UK. Blood group, dietary needs-vegetarian- and a note about an orthopaedic mattress seem to be a limited summary of this inmate. Pearson remained irritated and watchful about not knowing.

Jacob organized the room of compressed cardboard furniture in manner that matched Pearsons mood and anticipated O'Dell's. Jacob reflected his continued disquiet about the previous hour through the amount of noise he managed to generate in moving two chairs about six inches. They sat and waited in what seemed like a railway station waiting room, silent but expectant. During this interregnum, Ruth entered his thoughts, fleetingly and without warning. He felt strangely curious about her remarks earlier. He was unable to delete or even file them and so their disposal was beginning to puzzle. His stare at the windows revealed the fact that they could easily be opened enough to allow the passing of a small person. The irony of a high security segregation block having a window that opens was not lost. An entry into the log of maintenance might be required.

Hearing a muffled 'in here', the door opened and in walked O'Dell. His entry was anything but gladitorial. He was small, very plump and unkempt and possessed a redish tinge to just about everywhere in which his skin was visible. He looked nervous with two very apparent stains under each arm and with the slightest eye twitch; he conveyed a real sense of unease and dissatisfaction. His mental health had already been examined several weeks before the move and was felt to be within acceptable limits but his presentation today may have that diagnosis questioned. He personified what years of custody, poor food, no exercise or sunlight could cause. Unshaven, wearing odd slippers with one sock, he located a chair into which he slumped, expelling air from his mouth that suggested imminent diabetes such was the foulness of his breath. Slowly he removed his spectacles and with the care of a jeweller searching deeply into the quality of a presented gold ring he inspected each lens, firstly licking each piece of glass then using his handkerchief to remove any remnants of moisture. At the point Pearson felt able to introduce himself, O'Dell paid no regard to the opening platitudes as he remained dissatisfied with cleansing process. So much so he repeated the ritual again. More licking and rubbing, holding the frame to the light to inspect. Repeated again. His eyes eventually found Pearson and he locked into the current that was moving between them.

'Thank you for agreeing to see me. I gather you are a busy man but to find time to come into this unit is very much appreciated'. O'Dell's accent was that of a Northern Irishman, denoted by the harshness of the sentence structure. Looking almost a characture of his countrymen, this extended to the charm that radiated from the majority of citizens from that part of the disjointed kingdom. This surprised Jacob who looked up the moment the words interrupted the quietness. He wasn't sure what to expect but the demeanour of O'Dell did not fit into his mind set.

'You will quickly gather that I have rarely spoken with the prison authorities or at least with those charged with maintaining it so it is doubly appreciated.'

Pearson was receptive to the tempo that had been set. The fact that O'dell stopped again to clean his spotless glasses again seemed unimportant or at least not viewed as some elaborate ploy to arrest power or to seek control.

'I am not about to complain about the move. It was unnecessary but I had little say in how these judgments are arrived at. I could have done without the travel sickness, however. I hadn't been in a vehicle for years it felt like. Hence the way I look. It reflects the fact I still feel quite unwell. No bother.'

He went quiet and stared hard at Pearson assessing the extent to which he was being attentive and actually listening. As always it was never partial. Pearson felt no urge to make a comment other than to passively invite O'Dell to continue. Jacobs' relaxed state was evidenced by an unimpressive array of gothic doodles.

'The staff have indicated or at least made the point that you are fair Mr Pearson although one wonders if this is an overrated virtue. However I have a request or a demand, to be more accurate to make if that doesn't sound too rude'.

Pearson allowed the gap to ride a little longer than O'dell anticipated and took that as indication to continue.

'I would like to be transferred back to Ireland, to complete my sentence there. The basis of this request is rooted in compassion.'

His features never changed. Jacob's instincts were to question his nerve, inwardly.

'I have a daughter who has been diagnosed with Leukaemia with the prognosis being very poor. She can barely walk and my wife's responsibilities must be with her.'

O'Dell never wavered in his dispassionate commentary although his glance at the table when he mentioned the diagnosis was the only indication of some internal change of mood. He made a supplementary point about the family doctor could be contacted to verify his daughters condition as could the family priest. Names were provided complete with addresses, phone numbers and so on. Pearson, interestingly never doubted for a moment that he was speaking anything other than the truth. He doubted if he had the capacity to use a daughter as some form of shield or ruse for an elaborate escape. Pearson often felt his only virtue was an ability to hear the truth when it was spoken. O'Dell continued.

'I gather the transfer criteria are being relaxed given the point to where the talks have reached. It is ironic that at this late stage, we political types are seen as important. Whatever the position, I am making a simple request on your service and hope you can find it within yourself to make the necessary representations.'

His reference to his political status sounded flippant-uncharacteristic of his type although fleetingly, felt this to be a little judgmental. The glasses ritual was again resumed as he slouched over the table complete in his request but realising that any answer would not be immediate. His ordinariness became more evident, paradoxically. The secondary reaction was that his request, laden was trauma and pathos would be rejected in minutes even if he had a prima facia case for help. Provisional IRA do not have the political cache of a middle eastern brother. They were often viewed as shrill and without class. North Africans and those further east had political currency, quietly spent by the foreign office when the need suited. Pearson looked at the names of the priest and the Doctor and flicked to page three of the file then looked up.

He caught the mood of O'Dell who looked lost and without balance.

'What I would like to do is to firstly read all your papers and clarify who you are. This isn't some ploy to disregard your very real plight but if I am to make a case, I do not want any surprises to be thrown back. You will understand the formalities involved. I will also contact these people to whom you have referred and I will also speak with your wife if that is acceptable.'

A flick of the left hand indicated that it was. The suggestion that they would meet tomorrow at a similar time was also appreciated. They both stood up, O'Dell talking as he reached his small, indifferent height.

'I have no choice other than to await your response and I will be patient. It was good of you to come, thank you and to you, the quiet one.'

He smiled at Jacob who was still sitting, looking awkward. He shuffled to the door, opened it, allowed others to step forth and returned to his cell.

Pearson made a note for one of the officers to locate the full file which would have travelled with him on escort. A short discussion of no importance with those around at the point of exit from the unit filled a moment as this small group made its way back to the administrative block. Work was concluded for a short time and lunch with Ruth was anticipated.

Chapter 4:

The space that surrounded Pearson and the handsome Ruth as they walked to the 'mess'- an entirely accurate description for what passed as a place to eat if not savour- was filled with tension. The talk was smaller than usual and even their respective stride patterns appeared out of cinque. Neither were at their most fluent in differing ways. This heightened Pearson's sense of something not being as it should and that maybe a situation had developed during the morning to upset his colleague. Or perhaps she was sitting on some personal news about which she needed to talk. The curiosity within this encounter was made even more alive in that Pearson too felt edgy, un-centred and far from relaxed. The morning had been taxing but unremarkable even allowing for his now diminishing annoyance for not being consulted about the O'Dell move. The relationship between this thought and the decision making needed to resolve the issues that had arisen were familiar but not without demands. Consequently, he concluded that what Ruth was about to discuss required close attention and was about certainty not work related. He was not proved wrong.

A table was located amidst a noise usually associated with a large canteen. Strangely, this made it easier to talk. The positioning of tea cups and sandwiches closed the superficial distraction that prolonged the non-talk. Eventually, Ruth commenced.

'I really want to apologize for the message I left on your answer machine last night. I feel foolish and it seems so pathetic what I did, particularly after a night of no sleep. I'm almost embarrassed'.

A smile flashed across her face that implied that neither of them felt a need to feel coy or sheepish in each other's company. She continued.

'I hadn't even been drinking but I simply did it as a matter of instinct. You must think I'm a complete tart but I did what I did. It's been coming for ages I suppose and I have few real friends, none of whom I was prepared to talk with, at least. The "you always seem so happy" platitudes are not what I needed to hear. It was a need to talk to you or at you that was required-coming over would have made things worse. So, when you never really acknowledged me this morning I simply assume you were either put out or you were being more android than usual. A little unfair, sorry, so hence the need for this. Before you go bonkers about O'Dell, I was the duty dog on Thursday when the call came. I insisted on the file coming and I simply forgot to tell you. Please don't shout- an indication of where my head is. I'll say sorry once more and let you calmly reflect on my ineptitude.'

She was many things but never inept. Pearson's eyes never left Ruth's, allowing the words to drift through him. She is a curious sole, he reflected. Wonderfully able and direct, assertive, clear and reliable. Peer beneath the surface and you find a vulnerability of spirit, an indifference to self and the qualities others see. She had no idea how good or indeed potentially beautiful she was. Perhaps this last quality was of no importance. He always sensed the effect she had on men, especially those of a particular age although few would dare concede. In these few minutes, Pearson perception of her was confirmed, concluding that here was a colleague, now a friend whose trust was innate. He felt unable or unwilling to think about why although a thought moved that posed the question of why today. He hadn't even heard the message and yet he filled in the gaps. She had broken, almost, from her partner. He sensed that she liked him and used the most recent episode of unhappiness as a pre-text to call. Why not? He suggested that it really was alright. He invited her to put away the embarrassment or at least park it. He then suggested that she talk some more, suggesting intrigued to think that she felt he could help. His look endorsed her need. A glance implied that if he could help, he would.

'I knew you would be aloof but thanks.'

The awkwardness of trying to eat and talk was forgotten. Mouthfuls of churned lettuce moved around, unabashed. She continued, a shade to quickly that resulted in a coughing fit that attracted some unwelcomed back-slapping. She continued, again.

'We argued, again- an absent feature of our previous years which indicated the lack of interest. He became weepy but more to the point, I didn't. I felt pity and anger at him for crying, he looked so weak. He left the house mid-afternoon and I just needed to talk to someone, straight with no axe to grind or vested interest. The bit about valuing you I'm not apologizing for. I just hope your wife doesn't here it.'

Unlikely he thought. They affected an unconvincing laugh and on cue he moved the subject forward but not before a silence entered the space between them and so defining the moment. Their relationship had changed or so Pearson had thought and of course, wished.

'O'Dell?'

'Odd. Phone call late Thursday night. Usual stuff about security risk, escapee potential. Irish type who was being difficult. A very long saga about his behaviour in the Full Sutton special unit. Subversion was mentioned but the evidence was a bit light. The lay-down order needed ministerial approval but it came through. We had a slot- agreed on a 28 day order. He arrived. I met him briefly but didn't want to talk although he was polite. He said he had no idea why he was moved and said he wasn't consulted which was a strange thing to say. Said there was an issue but wanted me to read his papers. His file arrives and it's the thinnest thing you have ever seen on a guy who has done seventeen years or so. He has barely spoken to anyone. Never asked to see a G grade or even a priest. His recent log made no mention of wrong deeds. His appearance and demeanour do not match the perceptions, at least not when he arrived. All the papers, the confidential memo, the lot- all on your chair.

' Offence?' Pearson's work mode had returned.

'A bomber. In and around Belfast mainly but was shipped over here for his own protection six years ago when word leaked that he had informed on some big republican noise. Nothing on file- I got that from your opposite number on Saturday. He seemed quite resigned really and I doubt he will present our seg any real problems.'

'He asked to see me this morning'

'What for? On application?'

'An issue about his daughter being unwell and wanting to transfer back to Ireland.'

'He's got no chance. Besides, he would be putting his life in danger. How strange'

'I'm about to commence the digging this afternoon. Not optimistic however. Not unless he's got any new information.'

'I am sorry about last night.'

'As I say, park it. Besides, who else phones me?'

Lunch was concluded and they returned to their respective domains. Pearson always carried the air of the slightly remote, the troubled man about whom little was known. He joined nothing and yet he moved amongst his charges with ease. The gossip turned up little from previous jails other than he was sound, liked and trusted. His canvas, the one that was visible, had only background. No detail.

Clearing a back log of messages and signing the order to remove Khan, Pearson too was struck by the thinnest of the official file on O'dell. He had never met any type of political who was nothing if not polite or articulate, well mannered or reasonable. The relationship between the crime and their being seemed incongruous. The members of the IRA were no different. Discussion was limited to Rugby, Joyce, the Test Match or the developing economy in South Africa. Talk of the troubles, the politics of division or the historical perspective, was rare. References to it being very sad and the ruination of good people were more common. The prisoners never placed a single demand on the prison and would refuse to cooperate with any official reporting activity but always politely. The paradox being the mayhem they caused and the subsequent behaviour when in prison. O'Dell was no different. The buff folder neatly compartmentalised his life into five sections. Background and personal information first; social and family second; Prison and institutional details next, very thin. A third of one modest sheet revealed a man not dependent. Security reports and records of all approved visitors and an on-going schedule of visits. Nothing remarkable. Other than his wife, three children and her parents, only one other visitor had been approved. A priest, Father Mackean, who had visited each Christmas since he came to the mainland. Security reports, nineteen in number, indicated that he was an unremarkable prison career to date, isolated from other IRA members having, apparently, renounced violence as a legitimate part of the cause some six years earlier. It was evident that the recent bout of service anxiety was in effect the first, thus making his move all the more unusual. Pearson thought he would consult further with his colleagues to either clarify or corroborate their concern. The health section illustrated an ulcer, peptic, in 1982, heart palpatations a year later, gout in 1985 then an apparent few years of calm. 1990, February, heart attack, very serious. Life threatening; which may have accounted for the denouncing of violence. Although he recovered, he endured a further scare twelve months later. Since when, his health has generated no further concern. The notes reveal a poor diet and personal regime of no exercise, accounting for his pallow, overweight demeanour. His eyesight is acknowledged as being poor and he needed his wisdom teeth removed. The concluding section contrasts the confidential memorandum; a document that pieces together and then summerises in some nine pages, the details of the crime and other information.

In the measured, understated sentences of the Home Office, a detailed précis of who O'Dell was, what he did, the consequences, what the presenting evidence revealed and the trial tested. The judge's comments when passing sentence were also sectioned as was the few strained remarks made to the officials of the executive. The projected and anticipated length of time to serve and a comment about where O'Dell was located within the IRA command structure brought the document to a stark conclusion. Pearson commenced his reading with no little indifference to that which acts as a real disguise for what is a very clear mind that is able to retain substantial detail. Ruth enters his mind fleetingly then leaves again, having heard the apology once more.

O'Dell's life was neatly unfolded for the now focused reader. A birth in 1950, an only child, the passing of the eleven plus, the death of both parents within five weeks of each other when fourteen. The completion of seven O levels and three A's opened up a route to Queens in 1969. He refused a place, instead taking a job firstly with an insurance company, then with the Belfast city council in the surveyors section. His career progress was measured if unremarkable, completing his professional examinations and entering his list of chartered practitioners when aged twenty-four. His work appraisals and the informal testimony of colleagues indicated that he was a quiet man thorough in all what he did but he was never at ease with the harsh world of contractors and construction workers. His lack of personal presence and leadership qualities coupled with a poor standard of personal presentation- a feature of regular comments- meant that a management position was unlikely. He never challenged this view and often conceded that he found routine judgements on different tasks difficult. Time keeping was always precise and he was viewed, in professional terms, as sound if unimaginative and always cautious. He lived in Ballymena, a small town north of the city and commuted daily by bus. He never drove. He married when aged twenty seven, a local divorcee and had twins some nineteen months later. Colleagues mentioned that he was not fazed by this experience, simply going about his work without the usual signs of tiredness. Christened a catholic, confirmed when eleven and taking his first mass soon after, church attendance stopped once his parents died. He claimed that he saw little purpose in the rituals of a religion he thought was dying. His external world was that of diligent functionary who took pleasure in his work that included helping in the redesign of the city outer ring-road and a small section of the Derry link.

The ordered existence of the city council employee masked an alternative world that had at its centre a murderous philosophy designed to provoke political change and achieve certainty. O'Dell joined the IRA on his Eighteenth birthday. The limited intelligence reports put together after his emergence illustrated reasoning for embracing violence simply because he felt his country was occupied. He had read accounts of Scott, Waugh, Trevelyan, Joyce and Shaw and the political memoirs of Churchill and Lloyd George by the time he was sixteen and all had added to his rationale. Informers within the intellectual arm of Sinn Fein suggested that his republican views were not overtly developed and he never presented arguments against unionists or unionism. His interest lay within historical accounts, based on the imperialist power and its abuse, encouraged an inner belief that it was intrinsically wrong for any nation state to be occupied. He thought Collins logic was deeply flawed but saw his assassination as a political mistake. Allied to his resentment was the emphasis placed on religious classification. He apparently walked out of his interview at Queens when asked if he was left or right handed, code for the Church of Rome or Canterbury. Legend has it that he roared at the selection board that those who seek to ask such questions have forfeited the right to an answer. Neither his parents were involved in any form of political activity nor his extended family, such as it was, had no pedigree for allegiances with Republican thinking.

He joined a brigade within central Belfast and was appointed as one of many intelligence officers. His main duties were to listen to conversations within various pubs and places of social gatherings or to watch movements of a given individual and to report back verbally, never to write down anything. Indications from others suggested that he found this work dull given he never received any information about what anyone actually did with it. However, he was put to sleep in a department that would be of use at some point. His eventual knowledge of the planned road building contracts was used to enable large contractors who employed Catholic's to put pressure on city councillors for advance tender specifications but only in a limited way. In 1975 he was police vetted and cleared to work on the Belfast to Newry trunk road that included some advance design work on lay out, sympathetic for road blocks and other calming measures. This project also provided access to Military personnel who were seeking emergency approval for temporary access routes in and out of Army bases, being created in the South and West of the city. The plans were of limited value but they gave advance indication of where camps were being planned. This in turn would aid future mortar attacks or firework displays as they became known. By avoiding any political association with the political wing of the republican movement and maintaining only one discernable friend with whom he played chess on Wednesday evenings, he attracted no interest. His work reports were thorough and timely, uncomplicated in presentation. He failed to raise even the most rudimentary security concern when dealing with officers and civil servants linked to the ever increasing security presence.

Contact with his IRA handlers progressed seamlessly throughout the majority of his years of association. He impressed many of the more strident aggressive senior officers who found his quietness and lack of active rhetoric strangely calming. His contributions to covert activity were always strategic, having an almost forensic approach to planning: plotting times and exit routes when an opponent was to be removed. He was spared the ritualistic initial blooding of a sectarian beating or worse. In fact he made it known that he could not physically hurt anyone, even with a weapon. When present at an interrogation of a known informer he was violently ill when a death sentence was passed. However, he persisted in his commitment. At the infrequently convened brigade meetings, he said little although would always reassert his recognition that peace would only remain a fantasy unless his land was unoccupied. He would drink orange juice, always stand a round of drinks and would leave at the allotted time promptly, to catch a bus home. His wife new nothing of his allegiances; the consummate father, concerned and involved.

The phone rang, Pearson answered in irritated haste, to be updated about the errant officer who took pleasure in causing pain. He was to make a voluntary statement to the police and acknowledge he was to be suspended with immediate effect. The procedure would be followed and he thanked his colleague. Jacob appeared from nowhere to offer tea, an opinion on O'Dell and to confirm his attendance on detached duty tomorrow.

Judge Henry Blandford was murdered on the 11th February 1979 at 17.56 hours. His car, a government issued Rover was exploded when travelling south on the Newry Road from the city centre. Judge Blandford, Irish but not overtly so, loyalist by breeding and instinct, was presiding over a trial of some perplexing fraud at the central court on the Crumlin Road. His legal career had followed a traditional route which included the County Circuit both in England and in the North of Ireland, taking silk when 39. He became one of Her Majesty's leading prosecutors during the early Seventies, gaining a reputation of indifference to detail and a poor grasp of legal argument but was a charismatic orator and a socialite, extending friendship and amiability to all people so long as they were not either catholic or in sympathy with the republican ideal. He enjoyed a period of local celebrity by helping to fund a new private school that enshrined in its articles of deed that it should not be either co-educational or encounter children who were not christened of the Church of England. He viewed such issues with a simplicity that defied his intellect. His career as a Judge was all but cemented having successfully prosecuted in several cases in which provisional members of proscribed republican organisations were sent to prison for countless years. All before the presiding Diplock courts and often before judicial friends. Such ambition helped seal his fate. This allied with evidence of collusion with the police.

The planning of his attack was designed to indicate to all members of the legal profession that they, along with the police, Army, Prison Service and selected politicians, were targets, especially those who formed unacceptable alliances outside of their domain. Blandford was a known Mason and was able to use his networks with the police to filter information to loyalist paramilitaries. In return, he was provided with the services of a local prostitute, delivered and collected in an unmarked police car. O'Dell's part in his murder was documented in the next section of the Memorandum.

It was suggested that O'Dell was approached by the planners in the preceding November. They talked about the targeting of Blandford, preliminary identifying a time post Christmas. They already knew that he was to embark on a lengthy trial which meant his movements would be following a regular pattern. Several routes to and from the court to begin with then the security would relax and Two journeys would be agreed upon. He took lodgings in Newry, preferring to reside away from his home in the North West at any opportunity, to indulge himself in his weekly treat. The assault, the planners felt, should generate a new sense of surprise so extending the level of fear and anxiety, adding to the lexicon of approaches in which fear and terror could be wrought. The placing of a conventional car bomb was too difficult given the vehicle was often taken from a pool and so changed. O'Dell was briefed with the tasked of placing a bomb in a drain over which the Judge would drive. The bomb would be detonated by spotters and thereafter, mayhem confirmed. O'Dell took the view that this was a simple task, uncomplicated to implement and fail safe in restricting casualties. It was recognised that the driver would perish and given the projected bomb size, any other vehicle within a Thirty meter radius would have problems. All what was needed was a degree of certainty that a route was to be taken at a given time.

In the January, O'Dell accessed the relevant drawings and targeted a drain sump that was strategically located near the road centre. He undertook a personal inspection one afternoon, checking the depth of the chamber and where precisely the car wheels would be at the point of detonation. The field research was matched with a six page report to the planners that dealt with traffic flows, light sequences, pedestrian volume and the likely impact of any explosion on the immediate infra-structure. The drainage sump was located within a poorly lit thirty mile an hour zone although had various buildings and dwellings either side in order to provide maximum cover for the spotters. He calculated the time sequence from the point the car drove over the sump, the detonation and what exit routes were available within a much wider radius. The conclusion of the task would take place four days before the planned date. Using a bogus worksign, he provided fleeting access to the sump by a brigade engineer who, within ninety seconds had placed an explosive to the underside of the Iron cover and left. The radio activation device would remain sound for seven days so further planning was needed to ensure the quarry was connected with. The eleventh day was targeted as a political rally was to close part of the city centre but leaving two principle exits clear. The Newry road was known to be the fastest route and with an expectation of excess traffic volume, it remained the likely choice out. With some ideally placed gossip about road works being set up on the Newtownards intersection, the date was agreed. Spotters were in place by mid afternoon.

Via coded messages planted at two public telephone boxes, all personnel were in place to activate the assassination. The judgements proved correct. Judge Blandford left the court precincts at 5.20 pm and some 30 minutes later was murdered. The explosion accounted for him instantly, arching the car Twenty feet in the air, landing on its roof and igniting into a furnace of melting plastic and metal. The driver was forced sideways out of a door that had disintegrated and whilst spared burns lost almost forty percent of his body mass. A passing dog walker died within a week, having been hit by debris. Several motorists sustained injuries, and a women lost a leg. The scene resembled so many others seen before. It was always the smell at explosions that lingered. The spotters having followed the plan with a surveyor's precision left the scene seemingly un-noticed. O'Dell was already on his bus home, heading north, catching up with news story at the point of arrival at home.

'Have you seen the news, Shocking. That poor man. That poor women. The dog. Oh my god it's awful' was his wife's contribution.

This was O'Dell's first serious contribution to bringing about peace and he felt totally indifferent.

In keeping with brigade regulations, no contact or acknowledgment was permitted for four weeks. All those involved were required to go about their business in a way as to not attract attention or interest. Those responsible ignored the national and international outrage- to kill a judge seemed to denote something truly wicked. Grave announcements in parliament and the raging debate on local radio were overlaid with images of the dead people's families and eulogies from colleagues. Irrespective of how people viewed people alive, they assumed a reverence when dead. Qualities and accolades were awarded where previously, none existed. Reputations where enhanced. Bravery and talent replaced limitations and weaknesses. O'Dell's position and routine remained unmoved.

The first gathering of the brigade and the cell within it who managed the spectical was convened eight weeks to the day. The mood was sombre, laced with flashers of tension that O'Dell found hard to read. A formal announcement was made that Judge Henry Blandford had been assassinated given he was a known enemy of the Republican cause. Condolences were offered to the driver, the dog walker and a subsequent motorist who had also died. The Commander then issued a further statement to say errors had occurred during this exorcise that must not be repeated. He recounted the army council's standing orders on retaining and safeguarding all material of a related military nature and so it was regretted that a major breach had occurred. O'Dell became almost physically stuck to his chair. What breach? When? How? He was unclear about what was being implied. A private meeting of relevant volunteers was called immediately to de-brief. An ante-room at the meeting venue was made available in order further information could be shared. A man who O'Dell had never met or seen before appeared in order to chair the discussion which consisted really only of a monologue from this man, who entitled him Commander Doyle. His voice, high pitched but authorative addressed the point in question. Five others were present.

'The Army council of the IRA wishes to make a statement to the loyal volunteers who carried out the assassination of Judge Henry Blandford. In itself, the operation was successful with the known enemy of all peoples within the Island of Ireland having now been removed. However, errors in procedure occurred in the aftermath of this action that will almost certainly lead to further activity by the occupying enemy Army. An intelligence report had been left unattended in a motor vehicle at or near the scene of the intervention. This report, held in a brief case was stolen Two hours after the attack. Its whereabouts are currently unknown. This report would implicate at least one if not two volunteers.' O'Dell stopped listening, although he was able to hear that the culprit of this unacceptable conduct had been tried before the courts martial of the IRA and punished, being required to leave Ireland within Twelve hours or face execution.

It was the map that would incriminate him, with its unique references and codes, linking it directly to his department. It was a fingerprint, a photograph almost of him planting the bomb, screaming out: please arrest me. His diligence and ability to communicate the most detailed series of actions had been usurped by the opportunist thief and now absent colleague, later to be found shot in his own shower, such was the anger of his recklessness. A discussion that disregarded O'Dell's presence ensued with impromptu advice and guidance being offered, all of which lacked depth or understanding about how he lived his life. He must leave tonight, go to Dublin. He should bluff it out. There is no guarantee the brief case would be found. Kids only wanted radios. They would throw the thing in the nearest hedge where it would remain for ten years and rot. No one would dare blackmail the IRA. A frightened teenager would play the hero and had it in. Eight weeks had passed and nothing. Work was the only option. Doyle simply said the volunteer concerned must make his own judgement. If arrested he will not talk with his interrogators. His handlers agreed that he continue the 'at work' approach but felt uneasy with their association with a man who everyone knew would be arrested. Nothing stays hidden in Belfast. Briefcases never rot. Like ghosts, briefcases and people are always handed in. Eventually. O'Dell's journey home acted as the paradox for what had happened. Had he known about the theft, would he have left before now or simply carry on the same as if the event belonged to someone else's memory. Is it now he discloses his other world to his wife or does he do nothing? His fear had been displaced by guilt, that curious emotion like no other. Guilt linked with betrayal was the most desperate feeling. He arrived home and followed his usual routine of checking his step children then his baby daughter. He stroked his sleeping, restless wife's hair and etched his way into bed where he wept.

The memorandum concluded with a summary of O'Dell's arrest, detention, trial and conviction. The police forensic investigation quickly centred on the drain and its strategic importance to the explosion. By pure chance, the brief case taken from the spotter's car was found in the front garden of a church elder that lived close to the explosion. The thief, who had taken it, snatched in a moment of dare, ran a few hundred yards until his energy drifted and so gave up, then simply threw it. The elder handed it to a member of his church, a security force member. Although very wet, it had not been opened. The documents were analysed and within Three hours, O'Dell was arrested in his office and went through the initial stages of questioning in a traumatised silence, induced by fear. He said nothing but his inner resolve had collapsed within minutes. Within Twelve hours, he was told that his house had been all but destroyed, his wife had been very badly assaulted and his eldest step-son deliberately scalded during the search.

'Always the way, you see especially when the locals are made aware of the fact that you have become an informer.'

Standard tactics he thought but the anguish was no less evident. His office had been systematically taken apart, former colleagues abused and threatened and his immediate superior, of Asian descent was also arrested only to be released without charge the next day. The ensuing months leading to trial was one of sustained absence from his family or anyone else. His handlers were very absent. At trial, he was convicted within minutes following a four day hearing in which the prosecution made out the most compelling of cases that made conviction inevitable. He did not react when a life sentence was passed only to look round to seek out his wife. She remained absent, living in a refuge, frightened and sick with anxiety. She knew nothing of her husband's other life. Since his arrest they had not even corresponded.

The memorandum concluded with several pointed observations.

'In the course of O'Dell's arrest and attempted de-brief post trial, he was questioned about a number of other related episodes of violence and subversion perpetrated by the IRA. The extent of his involvement remained unclear although related intelligence suggested that he was essentially a planner rather than an enforcer. Specific evidence is limited although there is some suggestion he was involved or implicated with the setting up of mortar attacks on the police stations at Castleragh and Newtownards in 1978. The abduction, torture and execution of (unnamed) security force members was put to him as a matter of routine, all of which he declined to answer. He was offered the chance of safe informer status but he declined. Throughout his trial and in the aftermath, he said nothing. Conduct consistent with his training with his membership of a prescribed organisation. In this regard, it was felt that his overall status was limited in respect of formal rank but high in influence. Consequently he must be viewed as a highly dangerous and active member of the provisional IRA and his prison allocation and Catogory A security grade should reflect this. Upon sentencing, Lord Justice Short made the formal recommendation that he should serve a minimum of Thirty Years, with a full note of the judgement set down for the Lord Chief Justice and Home Secretary, who endorsed this view. His first review would be considered at Seventeen years.'

Pearson, oddly, felt the need to speak further with Ruth. He closed the file and felt fleetingly aggrieved, childishly, that his Tea was cold.

Chapter 5

The previous day's encounter with O'Dell disturbed Pearson's sleep pattern that was already fragile. He was hoping that by Eleven this morning, various messages would have been dealt with in preparation for an agreed visit to him some Two hours or so later. A run, a slow jog that seemed to take an age but was only Twenty Seven minutes, some fruit juice, no solids, a shower and a hastened drive had managed to create a heightened sense of interest in the day ahead. Indeed it was to be similar to many others except for its un-foreseen outcome. Ruth was absent from the morning glory. This was immediately regretted by Pearson. Wanting to see her had not quite left him from the Twelve hours previously. More internal interest but nothing more.

The messages in respect of O'Dell, four in total had been neatly chronicled by his Principle Officer. O'Dells' daughter was indeed very ill with a terminal condition. The prognosis was poor .Three separate sources had corroborated the condition for the nineteen year old; including the college principle who strangely paraphrased the line 'we all reap what we sow'. And this was from the child's elder. How necessary was this thought

Pearson. She was currently in hospital with a projected life expectancy of two months, maybe three. The third message seemed to confirm Pearson's suspicions that he was moved due to some internal 'repositioning' of the Governors authority at that end. The message suggested that no other data existed to justify the move and so it should not be viewed as having a bearing on any future decision making. The other message was a combined 'communication' from the Northern Ireland Office who in different ways confirmed the impression that O'Dell was a small and quickly rusted cog in the IRA internal workings. His move to the UK was due to dubious intelligence that he was an informer, later to be denied and withdrawn. The substance of the messages was that there would be a risk were he to return. Surely he must be aware of this? His wife had rebuilt her life without any assistance from O'Dell's associates and was coping well. The relationship between them was cordial but lacked the usual fervour and passion of the romances forged within the troubles. She had found it hard, granite hard, in the aftermath of his arrest and the pressure applied by the security forces on one hand and the complete indifference by his brigade. She had retrained as a nurse and had moved further into the North.

The Junior Ministerial reference to O'Dell was guarded and non-committal in respect of repatriation. The peace accord, whilst advanced, had not agreed a protocol for dealing with prisoners held on the mainland. Family hardship and the over-riding and compelling 'welfare criteria' was viewed as an irrelevance. If a prisoner had been moved to the UK for any reason a return to the North of Ireland would only be considered as part of a political objective. This wasn't even an answer thought Pearson although it implied a substantial rejection.

A short discussion with the Governor was uncomplicated and warm. They firstly discussed the movement of Khan and the nature of the allegations on D wing. The police had interviewed the officer who had, remarkably thought Lionel, resigned having 'told plod everything'. No union deputation or anything. Very neat and so very guilty, naturally. The presenting preoccupation was that of the press and whether the police would leak. So what? thought Lionel. Hardly paragons themselves. Ask every other Irishman on Alpha wing. Looking unkempt and sounding flippant, he asked about O'Dell and his seeking of clarification was real. He listened with his eyes to Pearson's resume, interrupting to jibe a colleague's behaviour in the squalid north. They would have seen this coming. 'The tykes moved him on some bogus pretext to avoid having to make a demand. Management by avoidance. Neat.'

He went on to ask simply,   'Do you think he should move, ignoring his security status and all that?'

'The usual checks have been made which indicate his bona fide's. The junior noise in the NI office has already bounced it but we could take it higher. Home Secretary needs to issue the order.'

'Permanent move or a roll over?'

'The latter'

'Makes it easier. Were he not Irish they wouldn't even look. Nonsense comment about political objective. The baby in the NI office is exceeding his authority by ten feet on that one.'

Pearson looked at this curious man in front of him. No longer making eye contact, feigning interest that disguised the paradox of an able mind, a moveable heart and a need to control. The fact that he liked Pearson and his selective consultations already meant that he was prepared to use some different levers for O'Dell.

'Were he not Irish and had killed someone through the usual motive of lust or greed then his application has a foundation. To see his daughter might help her more than him it seems to me. She didn't plant a bomb. Does the state have powers to extend the pain and suffering of a dependent? A nice moral conundrum. The dual impact of cause and effect'.

Pearson was unclear about what this last statement meant but sense the indication of support.

'When are you going to see him again?' Pearson indicated latter that morning.

'I'll see what favours are owed. Make sure your people are convinced it isn't some escape plan. Helicopters at dawn and such like. Make's my argument and its premise a little easier'.

Pearson was again accompanied by Jacob who was keen to provide a shortened and somewhat truncated version of Irish history. He also posed a question about whether the Scots had an equally strong case for creating mayhem. Pearson did not feel either interested or particularly inspired enough to provide an alternative thesis, preferring to concentrate hard on what he was going to say. The unease that O'Dell generated within him the previous day started to return as he moved nearer the segregation block. This in-part due to the fact that his news was essentially inconclusive. As he walked, he sensed that the prison possessed an air of industry. The reaction to the Khan move reflected the well managed nature of his exit, which was minimal. No further reports had been received that morning which had created space to complete some of the more mind numbing chores required of those who worked within a professional beaurocracy. Statistics needed tabulating, budgets agreed; a dynamic security strategy needed amending. All seemed secondary to the task of the next hour, however.

O'Dell entered the room, again perspiring heavily and sounding breathless when a muted 'hello' faded as the dominant vowel went unheard. He appeared to have been crying or exercising strenously although the latter was unlikely. He sat down and immediately removed his glasses and again completed the sequence of licking and polishing, using his shirt as the buffer. The room was cooler than when they met twenty four hours before which set the tone for the opening exchanges. O'Dell caught Pearson's eye and paused. He settled his glasses in the groves each side of his small nose and ensured his hair was pushed neatly behind each ear. The element of ritual was again present but reading the mood, he allowed O'Dell to open. It took an age for him to commence and move from a rasping, guttural murmur to something that was more audible.

'I sense by the look on your face that the news is either bad or at best doubtful. I also sense that your approach to these things is such that you put in the required amount of work too, in order to raise the spectre of me getting bussed. We can quickly move on from the assuming I'm right in order I might reveal or say a few additional things I omitted to tell you yesterday and will not unless I do your internal intelligence a disservice about what's recorded on my file.' The difficult, complex sentenced slightly jolted Pearson. The reference to the gaps caused the first shunt.

Jacob was beguiled by this man and surprised by the level of courtesy and deference shown. Usually, all dialogue in prison is based on demands, delivered at high volume. Pearson, less so, was already thinking that O'Dell was about to commence some form of negotiation that required careful consideration. An officer entered the room, place three hot drinks on the table and left. The moment the door close quietly, he resumed.

'My daughter is indeed very ill. Your checks into her plight will confirm that, only weeks to live so I'm advised. I know not Mr Pearson if you have a child but the impact this situation has is considerable. I fully recognise that under existing prison service rules you are not compelled to move me irrespective of the gravity of my daughter's health. I suspect I know procedures almost as well as you but all I can re-state is a wish to see her, to allow each of us time to conclude our relationship. For her passage and the sanity of her mother, there is an imperative here, based on the principle of mercy and forgiveness'. His perspiration appeared to be easing. He resumed more quickly than anticipated.

'You would have spent time reading all about me and my crimes. No doubt. An undistinguished career as a terrorist don't you think. Hardly Ned Kelly.' The self mocking was uncharacteristic and unconvincing.

'You would also have met countless other IRA men who will view their world differently to mine. All that talk about their motivation for the struggle, the imperial state and all that politically driven angst. Most of them will not talk about the inner feeling of power and status that goes with the turf. The mythical image of a hero. Never buying the first drink. Joining the club so to speak has little to do with political change but more about being valued. Its goes to the root of their being. It governs and shapes their character but hides the fear. To feel valued is to feel alive Mr Pearson. And so it does with my daughter. I have much to say to her, most of it will be words of regret and sorrow. What she also needs to hear from her father is that I am sincere about my renunciation of violence. I also want and need to say that I detest the IRA and its flawed thinking and its political cousins. She will understand that they have the values of a chameleon.'

Pearson viewed O'Dell's remarks as old fashion. And what if she didn't believe him he thought. Allowing for their respective Grammar school heritage, their mutual regard for their parents, Pearson had already developed a regard for O'Dell's intelligence. His pattern of speech resembled that of a banging door, caught in the wind. Loud and soft, irregular.

'Do you feel you have earned that right Mr O'Dell? If so, how?' The wind had suddenly grown cooler. This intervention from Pearson, having lowered the temperature even further given the tone of the question, caused both Jacob and O'Dell to look firstly at each other then the questioner.

'You appear not to understand the implications of this renouncement. It is always perceived as a precursor to informing and that was why I was moved in the first place'.

Pearson, poised and un-hurried indicated that he knew but that retort hardly answered the question. He invited him to answer further. The perspiration started again and O'Dell sat quietly for a time. He started to talk again but was unable to deal with the substance of Pearson's prompting.

'There is no risk other than to myself were I to be moved. By definition, I must discount my feelings in respect of that issue although I do have enemies in Ireland. That is beyond question.'

The drinks had not been touched. 'And the second issue you claim isn't on your file?'

O'Dell shifted visibly in his chair and appeared to be perplexed by Pearson's harsh exterior, akin to that of an inquisitor rather than ally.

'The murder and my subsequent arrest appeared to encapsulate the foolishness of lives being terminated. An utter commitment to the process of completing the task and a disregard of membership rules linked with total stupidity and here I am. The IRA resents the English not for their occupation but for their ability to organise. The truth being that the Irish have a gene missing that prevents us from building and sustaining anything. We are a people who can start anything but finish nothing. What would have happened had I not been captured? More of the same, no doubt.'

Pearson was unclear about where this discussion was going. It was neither the usual demeanour of a fellow of the brotherhood or the behaviour of someone desperate. A casual glance at his watch however generated a much less mellow reaction in O'Dell.

'Do I sense the contempt of an English man in my presence?' The wind had caught the door to the point of its hinges lifting. It was his turn to change the mood further. They both allowed the silence to move around the room and then settle. A fleeting period of eye contact was replaced by a mild sense of embarrassment in all present. It is the way adult men deal with such things.

'My daughter will die, irrespective of whether or not I get to see her. My words, have no doubt, will ease her parting, not hasten or cause it. So now I'll deal with second point which I sense you are keen to get at.'

At last, thought Pearson, his cognitions having stopped playing tricks. The point was bound to be one of negotiation such was his desperation to see her once more. No blame is attached. Who wouldn't think like that? The demeanour of O'Dell implied that his next point was one of substance in order to tilt Pearson back into play.

'I have acknowledged the personal safety is at risk should I be permitted to be moved. I also concede that any trip can only be short lived and I will then be returned to the UK. I shall not argue against that. Ten minutes will save two hearts. But you being you being you Mr. Pearson, you want something extra in return for you efforts. It is stated in your unspoken words. You have formed a view of me, an opinion, and an image because your memory is playing tricks.'

'As long as you know what you are saying makes some sense then I'm sure life will be OK for all of us but I have no idea what you are suggesting. Neither will my colleague here. Perhaps you can make your point because nothing has changed since yesterday other than I am trying to help you achieve your objective. You can arrive at various conclusions about my motives but as I see it your request is a simple one that will either be granted or not. The more antagonistic you become or more suggestive that in some way I have a vested interest in resolving this matter then you are misreading me. I am actually very keen to help your daughter. She has done nothing wrong.'

Pearson knew that his comments were inconclusive. O'Dell was very keen to drive home his point or at least to make one.

'Nice try but can we both not agree this is a little personal'

'What is personal?'

Jacob put down his pen and radiated the anxiety of a patient expecting bad news. The glasses came off, and were licked deeply, first the perimeter then the central part of each lens and then rubbed.

'I thought I was going to have to use my history to get you interested in my plight. I did not reckon that you would try and help me. Perhaps I have been inside to long, eh? Not to think that people in your position will deal with things on face value. For that I owe you an apology. Could I have a glass of water please, the tea is cold. Jacob caught the mood and quietly left.

The wind, having dropped allowed O'Dell's voice to assume a more conventional timbre, although it was the content that induced a seering, driving pain, exiting from the base of Pearson's spine. Within a second, he became transfixed, glued, wedged in his chair as though he was being slowly and meticulously covered in concrete. The content simply collided with the delivery and its timing. Unforeseen and wretched.

'He was dead when we got to him and all I did was to help undress him out of his uniform. You might be surprised to know that all of us in the car were repulsed by what had happened. We both have a history Mr. Pearson although mine has a natural conclusion. As for yours, it has many parts to it that have remained unanswered. Well, in recognition of your efforts, I am providing you with a detail that judging by your expression you knew nothing about. I suspect what I have just said will cause you some personal dissonance or perhaps it will merely solidify your thinking and fears. If I knew more I would tell you but as we both sit here we both understand what my actions and motives were and are about. Look at the picture sir and then climb into it.'

Pearson's eyes moved slightly to the right, catching the developing drizzle on the now closed sealed window. The silence that had developed was fermenting into a sense of confused anger within him although suppressed. Undress and uniform; two words synonymous and appropriate in many situations except this one. His wife registered for a moment then left. Daughters of similar ages. Would they be friends? His eyes returned to O'Dell who was sitting quietly with his hands clasped. Jacob broke the moment and passed a jug of water with a plastic cup, eagerly received. It took the strength of nine people not to permit himself a further question; to probe deeper. But the dots had been joined and he knew he was in the presence of his past. A map had been read.

'I will do I can to help you see your daughter. As you rightly point out, no guarantees can be offered as to your safety but as I speak, efforts are being made to overcome various obstacles. Perhaps the timing of this request could in some small way bring about a wider understanding. I hope things work out, especially for your daughter's sake.'

The three men present rose slowly to their respective feet, placed the furniture back into its correct position and O'Dell was returned to his cell. Pearson felt the need to sit quietly and think. He also wanted to see Ruth.

Chapter 6

'Something had change. Can I ask what?'

The incision was perfectly timed and neatly judged. The previous hour had encompassed dialogue; about work and the routine that was familiar to each of them. As the waiter approached, Pearson puzzled look had more to do with wondering why a bill needed to be placed on a saucer. More coffee was ordered with no financial adjustment. Ruth looked very tired but retained that calming organized look that permeated through unblemished skin and clothes of an unfitted, yet high quality.

'In what respect'

Her grin revealed a sense of understanding that indicated no real need to reply but she made a neutral, casual remark which also required no need to respond. The coffee arrived and with an uncomplicated crispness a card found its way underneath the unread bill. The repetitive stirring became a focus for each of them. She felt no need to change the mood, which was unrushed and settled. Pearson spoke.

'In forty eight hours, my life has regressed and progressed in perfect symmetry. In two days. Odd.'

Ruth found the comment obscure. She reflected on each facet of the sentence, piecing them together, like a patchwork quilt.

'The progression first. Start on a high note.'

Her mood was light in contrast to his, which was changing, so manifesting itself in predictable ways. No eye contact. Broken, incomplete sentences and a subtle evasiveness that she recognised but felt unnecessary to challenge.

'It was good of you to come and I've enjoyed the evening.'

'So far?'

'So far.'

His voice appeared strained, lower than a few moments earlier. It often was when feeling as he did at that time; diffident and withdrawn, troubled and perplexed. It was as though he was unclear if his character and the manner in which it functioned wasn't in fact an act. A suppressed cameo of presenting as being in control but feeling anything but. And for whose benefit, he wondered even further? The wariness, the constant checks and balances being administered within every situation. Each segment of each day being responded to with a caution; measured and unforgiving. For now, however, he was deeply troubled and he knew Ruth sensed it. Her quietness during the twenty or so minutes and perpetual seeking more than eye contact did enough to keep the interaction open ended. No demands or rhetorical questions. What she did was to demonstrate a real interest and fascination in what sat uneasily around them.

Pearson summoned a grin.

'I never actually heard your phone message. I always delete them when returning to the flat and make a point not to play them back. I suppose I'm to keep wondering what you said.'

'Would you like me to repeat it- word for word? I don't regret leaving it although it had crossed my mind that you may not have got the end bit, such was my warbling.' Her remarks were delivered with a repeated crispness and a lack of regret that denoted honesty and a simple purpose. A half smirk appeared between them.

'There is no need. I've sensed something for a while and I guess I feel pleased that you chose me to talk with. Are we behaving like farts?'

'Probably although one meal in over three years away from the gaze of partners and colleagues is hardly what one might call reckless. Besides I like you and always have but that too is hardly an original comment. We are not here to talk of us are we? Since earlier today, you have looked unsettled and ill at ease with yourself. This is an observation based on the view that you deal with most things with a simple arrogance - earthquakes to complaints about food- all packaged and responded to. I guess your axis has moved due to something having happened either at work or home. Or a ghost?'

'A ghost?'

'The past and all that. I suspect it isn't anything at home or to do with your daughter or your wife as it would be your nature to return and resolve whatever 'it' is. You are a concerned and caring husband, loyal, not a loving one I suspect but you have an instinct for problems. So when you phoned earlier I quickly concluded it was a more local issue.'

A feeble joke was attempted about the Governor, designed to open up some new thinking or contradiction but it did not detract from the accuracy. This was an adult moment, not one usually shared by colleagues.

A question was repeated by Ruth that required a response. She was following the script, he thought and he second guessed her response to his next statement.

'People always get offended when asked if they can be trusted. Are you any different?'

A loud yelp filled the virtually empty room.

'I'll give you ten seconds to swallow that line. You Neil Pearson would not be sat here with someone you did not trust.'

'How can you be so certain?'

'How can you be so ignorant of your own personality?'

The smirks and grins, childish in their inception had given way to an even greater sense of relaxation, leaving Pearson almost embarrassed by what sounded like a cliché. A quiet apology was alluded to in the voice, inflected through a mumble. Should he say anything? Would it compromise his relationship with a colleague? Should he move the presenting issue away from Ruth through fear of compounding her sense of worry over her failing partnership? Fairness was more vital than sensitivity. Or should he just talk and pre-judge nothing.

The restaurant was due to close and both sensed that the evening was not concluded. Without awkwardness or inference, Ruth indicated that Richard was not at home and if whatever was present needed dealing with now was the time. Without threat, she made the point that it was unlikely or probable that they might share a bed but to recognise the consequences were that to alter. Pearson was ahead of her on this issue and implied that it might be likely and probable but not certain. That was sufficient for each of them. What he needed to do was to share his issue and respond to the response. The time, overwhelmingly, was now. The need to talk, to find some form means by which the past and present could be reconciled.

The drive to Ruth's house was conducted largely in silence. Respective partners were absent both physically and within the mind which was very freeing. The lines that were about to be breached presented themselves as being less linear than at first imagined. What had surprised him even more was how he had simply enjoyed being around Ruth, in her space, behind and in front of her. Next to her, part of her thinking. Being in her presence generated calmness and clarity. And based on what?

Moving around a work environment in which each contact or encounter was fleeting, the occasional lunch or short phone call. Sitting through meetings and grabbing a minute at the end to share a comment. This framed their relationship but did not define it. He concluded that the past few years were a prelude to what was about to be unleashed. There were risks, of course but should he retain the arms length familiarity or gamble with the unknown? Regret what you don't do or haven't done rather than what you have. Perhaps. And what if he were to fall in love? That unlikely but potential outcome of removing a few pieces of hidden furniture that by some mystery, sat between them. How might he cope when it, the shared togetherness, ends, as it would? It always does. Best not allow the furniture to be moved.

The distinctive sound of gravel and the placing of the handbrake a notch too few concluded the drive. He had not been here before and was struck instantly by the smell in the hall-way. The excessive order and cleanliness. A house where no children were present and without warmth. It was also vast. Ruth indicated a need for more coffee and Pearson found himself at her side in the kitchen staring at the floor. Ruth initiated a long and very tight embrace that extended beyond the kettle's click. Neither felt the need to kiss, just to hold and say nothing. It felt natural and without the self-consciousness they both assumed that was the hall mark of an encounter with a stranger or the strained holding of an aged relative or sibling.

'This O'Dell thing. Something he said or implied to be more accurate. I would like to talk and then outline what I need to do'.

Chapter 7

The base was a disused village school, commandeered, on the margins of an old Victorian farming community that had all but disbanded. United in work, pleasure and accepting of the high and low faiths, having quietly negotiated two wars and much more besides. None more so when in 1969, three children were knocked down by a car outside the school gates, driven at great speed by Military personnel. The vehicle and its driver neither stopped or reported the incident, choosing to drive on without regard or concern They all died instantly and no one asked questions of the priest, first on the scene having attended a meeting with the newly appointed Head, who administered the last rites to all three together, irrespective of faith. Mothers always said that from that day, the village lost something more than the children. A shadow of incompleteness descended and within months families were beginning to leave. The accident acted as a metaphor for the tensions that were developing. Argument replaced conversation. Eating habits and the different rituals of different families assumed an importance, to define caste and being. The result being a confused withdrawal further south or north. The Kelly's and O'Malleys to Dundalk, the Doyle's and Peterson's further into Newry and beyond. A high street devoid of shops and a pub without custom represents the paradox. As did the collection of small terraces and bungalows and the distinctive Georgian Town house, formerly a hotel set back from the main road, then a home for difficult children and now empty and boarded. The school, having once been the centre and grounding for generations of young people was now engulfed in the utilatarian garb of militirism. Wired fencing, radio masts. A barrier controlling movement armed and patrolled each and every minute. Playtime and assembly, sums and words had their place but for a different purpose. The village had no more than a hundred or so people left, aged and indifferent to the workings of the base or the context that gave it its birth. Originally welcoming, the faces within the school are now hidden, forbidden to leave or socialise. Movement is restricted to the occasional vehicle and the daily landings of helicopters, smearing the faded lines of the netball court which is no more. The cottage garden, pond, football pitch had found room for temporary steel walls, concrete, electronic receivers. 'Kit' for the task.

No more than twenty people worked here at any-one time, round the clock. Detached postings were of six month duration for junior ranks, nine for senior officers. Hours of bleakness gave way to the occasional sustained nerve wrenching event or 'project' requiring forensic concentration levels and skill. Its function as a centre was by definition, secret and hidden from all but the selected few. To those who lived nearest, they guessed and surmised but not with any degree of certainty. That it housed soldiers and civilians was enough to generate tension although having so few merely compounded the curiosity. The larger bases in Armagh, Down and north of Derry accommodated the resident enemy. This place lacked the scale, the presence of a garrison and so raising its status a notch. Only one local person had ever been inside since the occupation. Mr Mazza, a man of Italian decent who ran a local vermin control company. He gossiped in the pub, telling two tales that were humorous but unimportant at the time and of no consequence. Firstly, people were very nice when being shown round. Secondly the toilets were the original sizes first installed for the little people. Hilarity was engendered when images of fat General's, in uniform squatting on something the size of a saucepan. Nothing else was gleaned. Its faded value belied its task that was never more important. To some at least.

The base controlled all intelligence reports, before they were presented to senior officers, ministers and their civil servants. Data sources from various flows, the police, field agents, informers, anonymous phone calls, were collated and converted into targeted activities by the security forces. The reports were sifted, read, compartmentalised, branded and graded and then weighted. From which then would arise some action, a task, a focused project, carried forward in the covert world that dominated counter civil disobedience. This was administrative trench warfare rather than characterised by groves cut into French turf surrounded by steel wire and chaos. The net effect however was the same even if the scale and enormity was proportionate. Lives were destroyed or saved. Perspective was everything. The actions would determine who would be arrested, searched, questioned, held without trial or eliminated. Who was to be ignored, or allowed to 'settle', what phone to be tapped, mail intercepted, house to be bugged or detroyed; or both? The reports would ensure who could be trusted or sacrificed, what secrets leaked, what career to enhance or ruin. What business could survive? What blind eye could be turned? The routine stuff of intelligence activity.

The command and control structure was simple. The senior officer was that of the rank of Colonel. Each shift was headed up by an officer, one of Captain within the line structure. A Lieutenant, his corporal and five operatives, clerks of the rank of private but all of plus 130 IQ, single and destined to be the future WO1 and 2. Each shift was self actualising, controlling its work flows and report production. Shift leaders would ensure lateral continuity and make the strategic links between the data. The support staff of a cook, and his assistant, a nurse whose combined duties included those of a domestic nature and a man affectionately referred to as 'tools'. The make-up of the community was like all others; full of tensions and fun, routines and rituals. Its power and myth burnt deeply into the military lore. Careers were made during a tour, so long as performance never dropped below the exceptional. In the seven years of its being, it had dictated the political policy of successive governments such was its importance. It set the moral tone for dealing with a political issue that had only one solution, known but unspoken. Its incumbents, selected with the applied precision of a French polisher, knew all that anyone could know about the workings of political groupings claiming their territory through organised or otherwise acts of terror. Knowing who planted the bombs or who squeezed the triggers was simple enough. Secrets were currency for which no price was too small. With axes to grind and jealousies not relenting, names were always put forward. Knowing why someone might choose to do something or when was an altogether more complex problem to resolve. Merchant banker or grocer, Monday, car bomber Thursday. The base always knew who but this was never enough. Prevention via intervention was the internal credo and was the basis upon which its work was judge.

Material was delivered twice daily, all within sealed boxes. Photographs, papers, reports, tapes, film the occasional contents of a bin. Famously and strictly as one off, the internal remains of a dead sheep which, it had been claimed, had just eaten some important work. It was a joke, a stunt that was never repeated. The culprit, stripped of rank, jailed for three months and dismissed; being more than a sacrificial lamb.

The material or 'work' as it became known was distributed from the four main military operational centres and from the central police stations in Belfast and Derry. Work that had already been sifted and 'visited' by a senior officer was filed into discreet date order and then forwarded. In the past twenty four months, over nine thousand episodes had been recorded, putting the data collation task into context. The grinding monotony was symptomatic of the task and its enormity. With any task dealt with by the intelligence core, 'can't' was not an option, a forbidden term.

The base had constructed the principle rationales on which both the occupying Army and the incumbent police forces could co-exist. The joint protocols signed several years earlier, however, had largely evaporated, leaving in their place that worst of all sentiment-envy. The unclear and misplaced control structure, poor conceptually as well as in practice fostered the belittlement of rank and with it, any real degree of a joint approach. Officials did what they thought best, in isolation of strategy and cohesion. A free-for-all plan was what represented the method of investigation or prevention. This resentment resulted in community's divisions, piece-by-brick, first divided then dismantled. It was a decision taken by the Army to erect steel dividers in the Ardoyne, the Shankill, the Markets, only to then request the RUC to supervise and patrol the consequence. Their senior officers, never consulted, seethed as historically sound policing strategies gave way to armed patrol, evacuations of 'wrong' families and an observable lawlessness. The Army maintained that the RUC were essentially Irish in attitude, not British or committed to the values of the mainland. With coded language, the Army leaked critical information to undermine its host police force with an attempt to discredit. It worked. The consequence being that supposed colleagues were put at risk and the political instability compounded. This was Northern Ireland; a place that spent each aspect of the day as an opportunity to look back, to be pessimistic, to be the possessor of no interest in the tomorrow. A bleak place administered by limited thinkers and security forces that engendered anything but. How could anything remotely touch the generations of entrenchment, irrespective of the religious factors; an element always overrated by the local's?

Its output needed to counterbalance the political agenda. The stopping of all insurrection at source by whatever means, often anarchic in application but clear in the knowledge that the rule of law was the benign form only of social governance. The police supported the latter, trying hard to maintain cohesion and tolerance. The Army the former with a mixed degree of strained competence or a dismissive failure amidst the lies and recrimination. As work arrived, each shift applied themselves systemically to a pattern. Each element of data was matched, checked, cross referenced, logged and then collated. Each Clerk had an area, each shift leader a functional lead and a particular expertise. The concluding hour of each shift required each Clerk to draft a formatted report that highlighted commonalities that were filed to the operational Lieutenant. They would, in turn, piece together the important ingredients of each of the five reports. This would convert itself into an end of shift briefing to the duty head of base, the lead Captain for that shift. This briefing, when matched with previous data would convert itself into operational directives to each district commander, required to plan and implement a particular course of action. Or do nothing. For anticipated 'spectaculars', an additional briefing would be prepared for the commander of Special Forces to deploy whatever resources were necessary. Each day the pattern was the same. Communication was routed to the districts through military telex with the expectation that commanders 'in district' coordinated activity between each other. Dependent upon personal ego, local RUC were either included or ignored. Special Forces were embraced regardless. An assumption often found wanting. Usually, but not always. The base commander would countersign each report before it was sent and gave guidance to districts on priority when asked. Such requests were not as regular as he would have liked. He would also order the meeting of senior commanders for each of the districts for strategic planning of managing 'targets'. Otherwise, he donned the role of the consummate beauracrat.

The base feared two things. Fire caused by an errant cigar or a kitchen oversight. Or the outbreak of flu. A mortar attack, car bombing or an actual fire-arm assault barely received a passing mention such was the scale the outer perimeter security and radar surveillance. Flu would account for several people at once, placing great pressure on others to work extra shifts and with it, the resultant mistakes and oversights. Otherwise, the internal atmosphere resembled a mixture of the exam room during finals, a country pub when off detail with the recreational stimulation of a cheap hotel. The dominant noise was silence.

Recruitment was via suggestion with a senior officer reporting on the skills set of a particular rank within a local Core. Soundings were taken, unofficial vetting followed as the process of 'matching' was pieced together. Once an approach was made, to any rank, it was never refused. To work at the base was to set the individual apart from all others. More often than not each recruit was the anti-thesis of those in the field who would live in car boots, watch or work as bar staff, convincing the locals they were of them. Usually loners but not isolates, the critical ingredients was an able brain linked with an inner confidence that meant that when sustained and relentless pressure was exerted, they would retain an inner belief that governed performance. They would always deliver. Noisy pranksters or garrulous socialites were not invited. Neither were the introverted or excessively secretive. Individuals who could laugh as well as analyse themselves, but not out loud, were seen to be of the right stuff .It helped if they retained a healthy alternative view to what was the conventional thinking pattern at a given time. Thinkers were in, reactive doers were not. Each incumbent base commander would have the ultimate power of veto when new people were identified as suitable for induction. Three had been rejected at the final stages, one famously, for writing to an old school friend , a journalist, who promptly used his letter as the basis of an article that was published in his home town local rag. Two careers ended for the price of a stamp. Two other's were bypassed simply as Colonel Bayliss wanted more Women recruited, enjoying both their company and diligence.

Neil Pearson followed a similar route. Commissioned as a lieutenant into the intelligence core some two years previously, having joined as a private but identified as having ability as an officer, he established an unusual reputation as an easy going individual who managed to generate interest from both his senior officers and subordinates. The eye of interest stemmed from his perceptible integrity. The last of a generation that took the Thirteen plus, he landed at the local technical school despite having no great academic talent. Strangely, he masked poor reading skills by developing an ability to listen with unusual intensity. Determined study rather than talent or real ability saw him through his basic exams, deciding to enlist. His parents were unable to fund study at the higher level and he saw little value at the time. His father cried when he needed to say no. Piece work being what it was. He was never heard bemoaning his luck or fortune, ever to indulge in gossip or talk of others. Compliments were issued, without rancour or envy, and were meant. He never spoke of a past, an upbringing or refers to a problem, a relationship or a particular episode. His conversations or interactions were only ever one way, centred on the other person their purpose or that of the task. 'Mess' behaviour was always cordial and would deal with comments and remarks, robust and often intrusively antagonistic with an understated smile, so deflecting the intent. His re-known sporting prowess and any reference to it he found embarrassing but coped with the unintended resentment, the preserve of men who envied but could never emulate. He was a modest drinker, who managed to depart when the behaviour become excessive and contrived. He undertook, however, his share of 'ill' cover- the clearing up of vomit, the putting to bed and putting right indiscretions. His reputation for directness and clarity came when he was seen to challenge the authority of a senior officer, drunk and incoherent, by not permitting a night patrol to be deployed without suitable infa-red touches despite being screamed at. This was during his second week of his first and only tour in Belfast. His group over heard him give the intoxicated name an ultimatum that were he to insist, he would end his career. His request to rethink the order reduced the Captain, aged and suffering from the fatigue and stress of real combat, was reduced to tears. The name and address of a treatment counsellor found its way into the tearful and broken soldier's quarter the following morning.

He never offered opinions, gave personal advice or sought to influence discussions or dialogue unless his view was countenanced. On several occasions, senior officers dismissed the young officers' views as ill prepared and marginal as they often posed questions of strategy and purpose rather than quiet acceptance. Suitability 'fit' for the next promotion was already blocked on the grounds that he lacked assertion, an element of breeding and as one colleague remarked, he should simply talk up more. Leadership was not an issue but his style was. An observation he accepted with a quiet wryness given he was surrounded by endless men, all striving to be more extreme than the next in their pursuit of action. Their motive for decision making did not fit with his perception of what was required. He had become bored with the number of events he had attended as part of the post incident debriefs, when lives had been quietly wasted often due to, in Pearson's view, the stupidity of new officers seeking to carve a niche. He realised very quickly that his ranks were not in the remotest sense heroic or driven. So many had joined the military to pursue a trade or play sport, to travel and to drink excessively. Holding a position under fire with limited munitions surrounded by the heat and smell of chaos belonged to a different grainy image of Sunday afternoon films. Great speeches on the parade ground were moments in time. The sense of duty disappeared as soon as it came. Soldiers, he observed would put more effort into organising leave, teams, collections, great acts of stealing or pranks than in preparing themselves for potential death. And yet when the time came to act, they would always react to officers leading from the back. His accent set him apart from other young officers in the intelligent core. A neutral London, northern home counties voice, sat oddly with the Middle England, flat but measured public school vowels of division two universities; places where Pearson never went, to his constant regret. His only one. What he did manage to do was achieve the third highest percentage at his recruitment exam and subsequent board. Despite the misgivings about his separateness, he became a popular officer recruit and remained so. His passing out discourse commented that; 'It is unlikely that Pearson will sustain a long career in the military given he belongs to the tradition that is unorthodox and unfitted. Yet to deny his ability to analyse and coach others and to articulate an argument that generates a sense of discomfort in fellow officers must have its place in this Core. He will not antagonise but he will stop free thinkers or rigid beaurcrats in their tracks. Above all, he will question - a vital commodity but one which he will discharge with a perceived sense contempt. He has a 'street' quality that will set him apart from other fellow officers but it is a quality nonetheless.'

When he read this, his only reaction to his Commander was that he missed out one other quality that he knew he possessed which was loyalty. The reply made the point that loyalty was something that was displayed, not simply kept with the hanker-chiefs, and used. This response extracted a grin.

He never missed a birthday of junior rank, or a christening card and gleaned a reputation for never having delegated anything he had done before. Liked but never loved, respected but neither revered nor reviled. His curiosity factor, however, endured.

His interview with the base Commander lasted seven minutes, five of which lamented the Army's lack of strength in the set scrums thus leaving the number eight back peddling on their own ball. To be beaten by the Navy for the sixth year was too much to bear. The present company was accepted, with the young officer sporting the wounds of a ferocious encounter. The concluding sentiments switched to Pearson's new posting. 'Do this job well, please, for no one other than yourself', was an important reference to the isolated nature of the role. He arrived a few weeks later, on New Years day, to leave one hundred and twenty days later, the only ever member of the Core to resign a commission early, whilst on a tour. The endorsing sentiment of do it for oneself held.

Chapter: 8

Pearson arrived by helicopter, a journey and form of transport guaranteed to make him feel ill. He was permitted the standard issue of personal effect and working fatigues but no other belongings. What items he had from his relatively short career to-date were stored elsewhere although when put together would fill barely two suit cases. Having completed the two phase level of training at a simulation centre outside Cirencester he felt prepared and relaxed about the presenting future. Time at the Army's nerve centre in Kent added a dimension to his preparation that was more intense. Here, four individuals at any one time are trained in the techniques and systems used in the base in anticipation of their next deployment. Once transported to the what was known locally as the 'stadium', for reasons no one knew although the flood-lights perhaps provided some insight, full induction and live activity was carried out during a four week period, overseen by a 'leader' of junior rank whose task it was to work through all the sequences of data arrival, the sifting and filing. The report preparation was personally overseen by the shift leader as part of what became a daily four hour activity of instruction.

Pearson's leader was Corporal Simon Jacks; his shift leader was Captain James Gladwyn. Both men greeted him from the helicopter, the former with schoolboy sincerity, and the latter in the manner of an indifferent teacher, of Latin perhaps. Tea and cakes were shared with idle, stilted conversation about quiet holiday periods, orchids, the Cheltenham race festival, and farming, about nothing. This ritual completed, Pearson's room was shown first with other facilities second. The base was exactly as it was described. A series of small classrooms, a hall and the smell of polish and plim-soles still evident. His guided tour was a mixture of what was allowed and permitted, what wasn't. A brief meeting with and a discussion thereafter about what 'Sir' liked and approved of and what he didn't. Oddly for a man who suggested that he wore two hair shirts, he accepted that relationships would form and end, atmospheres created and tensions felt but he would never intervene. He asked that sexual activity was 'suppressed', a curious but necessarily accurate term. He felt his stance, understated in action and intent, would create a balance and a reference point for the demands of close proximity living. 'Navy can't cope with mixed company on ship of course but it's unnatural to deny the realities.' He mused. He reminded new arrivals that by definition, any relationship could only be transient but in an unguarded moment implied that they were often the best type. 'Arriving or leaving: both states have their pressures'. Pearson felt his views reflected the values of a wise and compassionate man, modern in all things except appearance. Or at least he hoped so.

His first full briefing was to be that afternoon with Gladwyn. Full minutes were to be taken, verbatim, which focused on the conditions of his deployment, the strict rules which forbid any external contact, an explanation of what was allowed in terms of incoming and outgoing correspondence and the required response to personal trauma.

'If one occurs that necessitates your departure from here, it will be under escort for no longer than Forty Eight hours. Any longer period and your posting here will be ended. That includes parental bereavement and so on. Quite simply, it reduces the potential for leakage or undue pressure being applied to either you or your people were it to become known that you were posted here. Harsh, I know but accept it. In other words, your time here is just that. Here. I assume I am not saying anything which you were not already aware of. No leave will be granted or requested and all telephone calls are restricted and monitored for obvious reasons.'

Pearson couldn't think of anyone who would want to phone him. Not anymore at least. Not for now. After the posting, he was invited to bask in the reflected glory of having completed the most arduous of experiences. Quietly he consumed all what was said or hinted at, and listened intensely for the gaps as Gladwyn read page after page of security directives, periodically inviting a comment but never really wanting one. Pearson's instincts, rarely misplaced or ignored, churned over whilst being attentive to the talking Captain. Within the timescale of about an hour, a handshake and the sipping of Luke-warm tea, he had concluded that he needed to be selective about how best to react to him. He was short in stature and possessed a slightly nasal timbre to an accent that was from the pages of an Evelyn Waugh novel. He had developed what became something of an unspoken habit of stretching out his neck and running and index finger around the inside of his collar, so affecting the suggestion of an irritation. Eye contact was fleeting which matched a somewhat restless, nervous demeanour keen to move the conversation on just at the point it was flagging. A pause that invited 'any questions' suggested nothing of the sort. It was an audible full stop. Gladwyn did not like questions, at least not from a source that was new. All aspect of what was being conveyed was largely briefed before arrival. Questions therefore suggested a failure to listen carefully previously. Pearson sensed something absent within Gladwyn. His hurried monotone delivery implied boredom but it wasn't. Anything but. The briefing concluded with a series of references to the current 'state of play' with the 'enemy' and the setting down of present preoccupations.

'We are expecting some significant episodes of activity over coming weeks with all indications being that the calm is to be broken. You arrive at a time of intense speculation about where the war effort is heading with an emphasis of a more covert enforcement strategy of targeting known terrorists now favoured.' Pearson winced at the Juxtaposition of the terms enemy and war effort but not visibly, or at least he hoped. He found this language contrived and lacking any sense of realism but of course recognised immediately that such views were rooted in his wariness of the person providing the delivery. By contrast, Simon Jacks presented as an uncomplicated individual, focussed and someone who could deliver his guidance and instruction in clear and precise prose with accuracy and without fuss. Rules were repeated, procedures accentuated, systems revisited. His accent, from the Black Country and so easily ridiculed, deflected from an internal presence that denoted steel and resolve that his external personae, that of an enthusiast, detracted from. Six months in, and just Two letters, sent by his mother and forwarded on, maintained the thinnest of contact with an outside world. He joked that he would experience more fun in a Prison and certainly more post. Yet the joke was unconvincing and not meant, such was his level of intense commitment. His demonstrated respect for the senior rank was sincere and punctuated different instructions with a bold and unequivocal 'Sir', underlined and felt. Pearson was often distracted from the training material given by his coach as he was the same age and as it turned out, possessed the same grades in their few O level's. A jack was an able, intelligent young man, full of goodness and cheer but not the possessor of leadership qualities, at least not to the Officer commissioning board. He managed to freeze hopelessly during both his exams and re-takes. His stated wish was to take the long route. 'I'll make it when I'm sixty'. More jokes, equally unconvincing. He produced endless tea, and boundless patience to limited and repetitive questioning from the newcomer. This last briefing concluded with a further meeting with Gladwyn who started on one of his substantial monologues, where comments were either sought or invited.

'About month three, you will feel at your worse, you haven't been anywhere for weeks and unlikely to do so for another twelve or so. You want to go. I refuse. You accept it but seeth with the injustice and often tedium of it all. That is the time to consider what you have achieved. Your time will end, eventually, you will gain promotion within the year and be dispatch to Canada to train failed Americans and colonial types in intelligence practice'. Pearson was trying hard not to interrupt as he felt too many assumptions were being made but it passed.

'You have completed your induction; you understand the role and the task. You will work to me and only me and if appropriate, you will be invited to site security briefings with other brass to take a note. You will not talk to Sir unless invited and your shift pattern will be the governing factor of your time here. Lead your shift as you would any team. Be directive, delegate, consult and instruct. Do not be persuaded to elevate every piece of paper to that of the Munich accord. You will learn very quickly that we disregard most reports and even those which will influence briefings often get junked at the last minute. You must decide what is real and relevant to place before me. I'll do the rest. If you are uncertain talk downstairs first, to clarify and resolve. Come to me as the last resort. You and I will talk but do not expect a social relationship or even a personable one. You are subordinate to me and everything about what we do is dependent upon that'.

A pause and a sustained look at Pearson disrupted the flow of Gladwyn. He then continued.

'The present position operationally is worthy of further discussion.'

'I haven't discussed anything current as yet.'

'As yet, Sir.' Said with an embarrassed half smile but meant.

'Yet, Sir. My apologies but you haven't briefed me on the current situation and neither has Corporal Jacks. Sorry to be pedantic but the reference to a further discussion was misplaced.' Immediately he made this interjection he wished he hadn't. He sounded arrogant, almost pompous yet sneering. To Pearson's surprise, a mumbled 'point taken' was offered. Gladwyn continued, having slightly checked his word flow, to re-gather his thoughts.

'I want to make five substantive points about the leading operators in this part of the United Kingdom; points that will impact on your work immediately.'

Part of the preparation at Cirencester was to read the various documents prepared by both the military and anti-terrorist agencies. Added to these reports were historical and political text, providing a wider canvass to distorted beliefs and absolute truths. Three novels were also part of the requirement. Pearson's recollection of the material being that it provided grounding to his appreciation of the intensity the communities felt and the fluidity of passion. Part of the reading included a profile of each of the top Two hundred or so operatives from each of the active paramilitaries, their family links and labyrinthine webs that were a feature of Celts and Anglo-Saxons alike. And all within a few, perhaps three or so square miles. Generations of families carried on the tradition of antagonising the government along with the various degrees of the continuum. What he also recalled was to view the struggle as being between coalitions. Catholics who never massed, Protestants who never sung or whistled the tune of 'The sash my father wore.' Territory, turf, work, districts, sport, horse racing and alcohol all collided with each stratum. Layer upon layer of similarities and yet it was always the differences that were shown. The Fienian intelligencer wanting nothing to do with the narrow world dominated by Farms that was the South. And the limitations that went with it. The class conscious workers of the North and East Belfast, wary of the London Bankers, wanting sameness. The Nationalists wanted anything so long as it wasn't British although blind eyes were turned when comforts were offered. The language of unification sounded dated and unconvincing when a glance at the estates highlighted drug dependency and no skills. It could be West Manchester or Newcastle or East Berlin. Everyone wanted everything so long as it wasn't permanent. Besides, violence generated its own economy. Protection, power and status, the arousal that guns generate. One other thing remained with Pearson on his list, his Pilgrims progress through a stagnant history of a mostly stagnant people. Funny but stagnant. The power brokers, the serial bombers, the runners, the drivers, the informants and the quartermasters were all men except three names. Men, all looking the same with harsh sounding names and all with a similar social profile. As a murderous group of peers, their commitment never faltered at least not publically. Neither grouping's within the list could seriously be called or viewed as Irish, he thought. They all owed allegiances to a mixture of Columbian coke farmers and taliban fundamentalists. Why did not more women offer a counterbalance, an alternative view? They didn't, so illustrating the shared image with an Iraq, an Afghanistan or Columbia.

'Over and above these points is an observation. Unlike most present day intelligence gathering, which is passive and non-committal, we deal with real events in which citizens, soldiers, leaders and criminals perish. Ironic really that all the hours of work put together by Five and Six, MI's to you, their net impact is minimal in terms of preventative action. I suppose our delivery is what sets us apart.'

An unsolicited silence was caused by a hurried glance at some notes that sat neatly in Gladwyn's lap. His uniform looked un-cared for and he generated the personal aroma of dampness. Not unpleasant but likely to become more so the closer one got to his skin. The whispers within the mess would suggest that Gladwyn took thoroughness and detail to an unchartered level. The base commander was highly dependent upon his analysis, particularly when 'brasses visited. Older than Pearson by some nine years, he affected an air of indifference towards the status of others by protecting his own. He had developed a ritual of re-checking the waste shredder pile before its eventual execution, seeking the hidden thread. He was more popular than Pearson imagined, using his range of risky jokes at the expense of some fictitious General. He once sang the whole of the first act of the Mikardo, uninvited the last Xmas eve. He started with point four, given, he said, its strategic importance.

'When that pointless phrase 'the troubles' is used, the conflict areas are essentially central and west Belfast, the main roads between Londonderry and the east and the roads south to Newry and Dundalk. Virtually all activity stems from these areas and is carried out within it. Just to make the point, that is where Ninety five percent of our data flows come from or leads to. Don't get seduced into thinking the problem areas are located or routed in the villages. They are not. Belfast is Northern Ireland with Derry being very second division, having never fully recovered from the robust policing on that famous Sunday.' Said with unnecessary emphasis thought Pearson, although the edge was noted.

'Point one, to start now at the beginning. We know who the top Two hundred movers are in this part of the world, as per your studies in Cirencester and Kent. Some die, so we top up the schedule from the second division. We also know what they are, where they live, drink, with whom they sleep, where they work, walk, play and bet. They always bet it seems. Knowing however is never enough or proof of any anti-social conduct despite what we assume. All internment ever achieved was the detention of nobodies. Each watch has access to the profiles of these citizens of the UK, and every time their names are reported on we build a picture. By about week seven, you will recall the dates of birth of all of them as though they were your own brothers and sisters or girlfriend.' He wished he had at least one of the latter, a musing that did not pass quickly.

'You can reflect on the significance of the fact that this very exclusive Rotary club boasts at least Two MP's, several priests, countless local worthies and a whole host of political officials. In one form or another, all adding to the grief and the social isolation of Mr and Mrs Ulsterman and Woman.'

His voice never wavered, with each word expressed with an earnest intent and sustained level of importance as a teacher might recite Blake.

'Point Two, you do not need to worry yourself about anticipated or known activity. By the time you have these pieces of information, the police and field units would have already responded. Concern yourself with new issues, new movements, tactics, places, new targets and so on. In your watch reports, express what you know to be new data.' His notes flicked back a page. He checked his thinking via a short stare at Pearson then resumed.

'Thirdly, codenames.' He reached forward with a note book, heavily soiled.

'In there you will find various coded names, used to denote political leaders, bankers, lawyers and members of the professional classes who embrace an arm's length approach towards the arm struggle, influencing here, touching there. All stand to make, out of this difficulty. The codenames change and assume a need to know basis. This book can enhance or destroy our work. Do keep it to hand. The final point relates to bogus data- wrong scent, hog-wash, nonsense and lies or worst still, half truths, all in the name of field intelligence. Try as we might, we never know who might go double on us but what field agents never know is who is watching them. I know as does the base commander of course but the one structured secret we keep here is the knowledge of who is watching who. One other person externally knows and that is it. I'm sure I don't need to make the point but if you sense dodgy info you tell me immediately, day or night. We have a mechanism to check the authenticity but such an occurrence is unheard of, only once previously. Massive hare sent running for what was a silly error, not a sinister one. As from now, you are on-side. You start tomorrow.

Chapter 9

The close proximity living was less problematic than Pearson first imagined. Food was plentiful and with the necessary adjustments of cupboard space, his room was moulded into the domain of a contented individual. Initially, the dialogue and companionship with others lacked depth but that was unremarkable in the circumstances. As the days drifted by, he concluded that as so much time was spent concentrating, tiredness and related stress mitigated against the more intimate relationships, plutonic or otherwise. Corporal Jacks become 'Jacks', his preferred handle. 'Makes things less complicated, formalities are retained. I know the drill. Your rank requires Surname or full title. Seem's excessive here. What Rogers calls a 'Win, Win'. They smile at the dubious reference to a shrink. This relationship developed with a pleasant tempo that enables both men to feel optimistic and to co-exist, to express differences, to play chess and to allow glimpses into the world left behind. Personal histories and school stories revealed differences and similarities. O Levels were the same, both regretted not doing French. Temperamentally, they matched. Jacks, skittish, rushed, eager to please but relentless when focussed and concentrated on a task. Funny, loyal and a limited range in jokes but a deep, penetrative mind on all things political, practically in his current role. Pearson, quiet, measured, unfazed or reactive, often laconic and very often seemingly absent from the discussion. His skills were more about listening than doing. Jacks was an early riser, a tea-brewer and an inveterate door tapper, bringing huge mugs of dark liquid and countless rounds of 'holy ghost', generously buttered and cut vertically so denoting his working class origins. He was a checker, someone who 'doubled and tripled', and always keen to talk, to debate, find roads into fantasy land, using tangents as a source of distraction, to pass the time. Every aspect of his work was thorough, of a style that belied his frenetic demeanour and image.

'Never considered applying again. Plain as that.' A direct response to Pearsons question about a commission. 'I know my weaknesses- the leadership thing really. Seen as too soft, too easy going, too happy to delegate all the big calls but I also know my strengths- a lateral thinker with a heart.' A giggle, almost, passes of as a laugh. The answer belied an inner intelligence and intellectual feel that wasn't readily apparent. Loyalty was evident. He was described by Gladwyn as the best 'blanket stacker' this place had ever seen by the country mile, a reference meant to be and was endearing. Attentive at all briefings and true to his own sense of self-perception. When a significant path was being tracked within a given line of data, he would order and present the information, make very detailed observations and then simply look towards the receiving officer and seemingly, not blink for minutes. His manner was unthreatening as was his presence. Paradoxically, he was listened to with greater intensity given egos were able to be parked. The personnel section would profile Jacks as a stellar intelligence Corporal. A performer.

'When?' enquired Pearson; a clarifying question to tidy up the specific date of Jacks leaving. Mid April, no later than the Eighteenth but likely to be earlier. I would love to stay but no one ever does. Germany next and then hopefully Canada. Exams to sit in September, Sergeants stuff. I'll pass the tests, will collapse in the interview and then receive the 'We are sorry to….' Predictable really. I don't really fit the bill for a field agent or a specialist unit. And I couldn't really train people, not properly. Just a good admin type really. Enough of this talk of me going, especially as you have only just arrived. Lucky bloke!

It was late evening and the conversation drifted around their respective careers. The TV was on but not watched and other members of the watch had long since turned in. Still the quietness dominated, punctuated by the murmur of radios. Gladwyn approached them both with an uneasiness that would be attributable to mores of a minor public school looking every inch the boy who was never invited to play first team. He mumbled a greeting, using the prefix for Jacks and the surname only for Pearson.

'Tomorrows trawl will reveal three things, allegedly.' He spoke with a certainty that did not match his posture.

'Movement is taking place in the southern part of Belfast. Four sittings have been worked up on player code four, Sean Devlin to you and I, in areas that indicate meeting points. The second strand to this is the person he was seen with and the locality. Thirdly, he made seven journeys between O'Connor's bar in the lower falls to a house in Newtownards in the space of three hours. This pathway needs to be tracked and re-tracked and cross linked to any related material submitted from the Londonderry site.'

Devlin was royalty within the provisional's inner sanctum. Retaining a profile of the working class sophisticate.

'Sir wants to wait until the last possible moments to cast the line, given all reports are indicating a significant piece of work. Delaying the cast, bigger the catch-hopefully you take the analogy. Check and re-check the data patterns and have your shift report typed and presented within the last hour of each of the next several shifts. Kabal meeting thereafter for the tactics and action stuff, latter this week. He moved away, leaving behind his dampness. No further comments from either party were felt to be warranted and so they drifted off, Jacks to read, Pearson to sleep.

*

The expected data didn't start arriving for five weeks. Each of the last nine shifts, however, spread across many hours grew in their intensity. The concentration turned each minute into dust. The spot-lights threw quiet shadows within the Operations room, creating distracting shapes, landscapes and vistas. Pearson would periodically drift amongst his team, offering reassurance, whispered and heartfelt. A veteran after what seemed like a few hours, quietly calling for thoroughness. Number plates, descriptions, the matching of times, sightings, absences. The paper drops were unusually light which was puzzling. Jacks started to build his chart: a montage of names, places, and colour stickers all transposed on a huge map of Belfast. Each data lead was mapped, checked and studied, all with the precision of a watch maker. No-one guessed or assumed what was happening, simply allowing the picture to emerge. Sir entered the room with the tread of the country vicar, the bachelor, smiling but saying little. He spent time in deep introspection, looking at Jacks' tapestry. He leant forward and peeled back a card to reveal a code name. His approach towards Pearson was understated, pausing to say good evening to each shift member.

'Lieutenant Pearson, I am sorry to disturb tonight's endeavours, thought provoking as it is.' This was a man of great courtesy, he thought, a curious mixture of Englishness and sub-continent subservience.

'Your man Gladwyn has asked for your reports to be submitted earlier during these past few shifts. I hope this encumbrance hasn't proved too onerous but to-day, I need to analyse papers by zero five hundred. There is every indication of something very serious being planned and a 'brass' briefing is planned at Zero Seven fifteen. I am sorry to press.' A fleeting glance was offered; a short smile then he motioned to move away.

'We have one desk to clear then I think we are about done. Without pre-judging anything, Corporal Jacks' jig-saw and the matched data indicates a potential car-bombing rather than a street or planted explosion. The point I am currently at would provide me with enough material to indicate likely location although the target remains stubbornly unclear.

'Politician we think but very uncertain. The next tranche of papers will be critical. I do appreciate your diligence and that of Jacks. Excellent cove, he is. He's innovated this charting thing, marvellous it is.So simple. He should put a copyright on it before I claim the credit, say Pearson? Good man he is, very good at chess you know. Always a sign you know of hidden depths. Can't play myself.' A snapped laugh left him and was replaced quickly by a smile. The benevolent Colonel, stooped, immaculately dressed and very keen to stand beside you rather than look at you head on.

Some three hours later, Pearson had pieced together what actually turned out to be a recognisable picture of a planned assassination. Different people with different tasks, weaving together an irrefutable pattern that would result in likely death. The report was filed at four, fifty eight, Two thousand or so words, concisely structured into a briefing paper, setting down each facet of the narrative so creating a sense of order to the information. It was held together by threads of certainty and small isolated pockets of assumption. Sir, having read it twice, asked for two points of clarification before owning the paper and its conclusion. The proffered comment of thanks was and sounded sincere. He continued.

'I would now like to ask if all shift leaders could convene in some thirty or so minutes in my office. Poulton may well have just started to nod off but it is important all are present. Doesn't happen often. Important, though. Captain Gladwyn will lead the briefing. As I say, important. Until then.'

Pearson took his leave and found himself feeling uneasy with himself. Tea, taken quickly, was shared with Jacks, drank whilst standing, propping up an uncertain looking partition wall. A quiet background of noise, generated by a mixture of paper and something ill defined. Distant aircraft perhaps. Pearson's attention drifted momentarily, but then centred again. Outside of the shift, it was discouraged to talk shop, particularly the specifics of data. The urge to talk was paramount so the convention was put to one side. For a minute at least.

'When it all hangs together like this, do you never wonder if it is some great counter ploy. The reports were so specific-Devlin almost reckless in his conduct. Frenetic even. I'm not sure if it's right.'

Jacks allowed time for the thoughts to settle, recognising that Pearson was clearly troubled by the certainty of the data. Settlement turned to drift and catching the mood, merely said that he too felt puzzled. His 'toy map' had come together in a fashion that would have barely tested a playgroup debutant. Or was it that all of them, inside and out, had merely applied the method. The results therefore should follow. He wasn't sure either and for what it was worth, he too was uneasy. 'Don't be late for the briefing.' Jacks was excluded and he hid his resentment, such as it was, well.

Sufficient time allowed for a short walk outside, amidst unkempt grounds of what once must have been a happier place. This moment was for real, sensing the rising tension of hidden feelings. The stuff of tomorrow's news, unless it was prevented, whatever 'it' was. He felt detached and was developing a sense of almost embitterment in that most men his age were not living their lives through the trauma of others. The absence of real pleasure in his life was beginning to grow. The detached, buried existence created an absence from women with whom he could confide, talk, laugh and sex. He missed them considerably, above all their smell. Base, perhaps, but true. Having completed the self analysis, he presented himself at the commander's door, a little early to assist in the preparation of the room. A helicopter eased itself into the required space, generating great levels of dust although the quietness defied the engineering. Two cars moved in and out, depositing ashen face veterans of countless meetings who found their way into a familiar if unwelcoming room. Coffee was tabled along with a briefing for each of the eight personnel present. Divisional commanders took their seats, the three senior operational officers, included a surprisingly relaxed looking Gladwyn, and with Pearson assigned to take a note. To be seen but not heard. The English Colonel opened the briefing, denoting the time, formal rank of each representative present. His urbanity created the necessary sense of calm although order, was unlikely to lapse. A freedom to question, to express, to rebuke was evident as was an implied code of deference. He apologised for the cups and indicated that the briefing would end no later than zero eight Hundred whereupon breakfast would be served. The next thirty five minutes was filled with an almost forensic account of the anticipated activity. Sir had pulled together all the variables contained within the reports and added his own brand of qualitative data. He highlighted inaccuracies of analysis as well as interpretation, pointed out poor street craft and named the field agent who actually used the private phone of a house in a republican area and actually spoke in English with a West Country accent. A tape was available were anyone wishing to raise doubt. He revised and embellished Jacks map piling on detail after detail, all delivered without a note, such was his grasp of detail. He concluded by making four specific recommendations and invited those present to embrace his position. No one said anything. The intensity was compounded when Sir indicated that his fourth recommendation might be viewed as challenging by the joint Chiefs and the Minister but he invited understanding, allowing time for a small joke at his own expense. 'Senility you see.'

Like a master bricklayer, each course had a relationship with the past and the next. For bricks, supplant words, texture, emphasis and meaning.

'Page Two of the report indicates the significant names involved in recent activity. Names one and three should be arrested and detained within the next Two hours and most certainly not released within thirty six or longer. Their absence will disrupt the logistics and will delay almost certainly the movement of the primed vehicle.' He went on, assuming that each of those present was following his unspoken logic. There were no dramatic pauses, voice intonation or specific emphasis of a given instruction. Just simple uncomplicated clarity laced with expectation.

'Within the next hour, the minister's PPS should be advised that his movements are to be modified as per the liaison protocol. Captain Armitage will action this through the usual channels.' An order denoted by a crisp nod followed by a furtive glance of the watch.

'If they have dummy drivers, the vehicle should be immobilised immediately. Live rounds are necessary. I don't need to elaborate. Critical that this element is managed without casualties.'

His eyes fixed on a man called Duxberry; a Major in Special Forces and the principle coordinator between the various functions to ensure his people are in the right place. The raising of the right hand, no more than an inch from its position on the table was enough to set in train various arrangements that would ensure marksman are placed within fifty metres of the proposed vehicle movement.

'My forth proposal is somewhat less orthodox but has merit I feel. This report and the related data to which I have referred speaks incessantly of Sean Devlin. I have no need to rehearse his previous felonies or to articulate his significance. He is the man of Southern Belfast and is instrumental in most things that are in-house.' This phrase was a reference to Provisional assignments, conceived and actioned within the city itself.

'It seems to me that the most natural action to follow is to also arrest him in the complete belief he will be untouchable. His removal from the area will be viewed with some degree of amusement perhaps but it will have little bearing on other events planned. What I would like to do however is to leave him floating. My rationale for this is borne out by comments set down on page seven which I invite you to re-visit.' Glasses were located in order a thorough read might be made. He continued.

'Devlin, throughout this period has developed something of an interest in making phone calls from O'Connors bar. Nothing unusual in that until you make the connection with whom he is speaking. Twenty nine calls have been made to the numbers listed. Interestingly, he phones the number, leaves it to ring five times then ends the call. Evidently some form of contact precursor and we have concluded here that it signifies completion of each facet of the planning but we are not sure. Importantly, the unanswered number is that of a London based financier, unknown to any of us. His role in proceedings is very unclear but there is every likelihood it is linked to complex structure of laundering and an Insurance heist. Once we establish a formal connection between Devlin and this person, ideally through a taped call, photograph or whatever, then we can move and lift both. An infra-structure you will note is in place monitoring our friend in the city. The overarching evaluation is hardly remarkable in that once Devlin has completed this mission, he will need moving, will require funds and so on and it is assumed this individual will assist. The financier has been planted for some time hence the data about the numbers but special branch are reluctant to speculate on a name until they are absolutely certain who it is. Having made a judgement about the presenting material my preferred approach is that we construct a scenario which implicates Devlin as a collaborator with the security forces and do it in such a way that flushes out the link in London. This could be achieved very simply by placing a coded message to the IRA putting up Devlin. As an agreement, force activity will be scaled down for forty eight hours in the Falls to allow some personnel movement as a quid-pro-quo. We would arrest some other low level types and make the bridge to Devlin. This will sign his death warrant of course but the objective here is to get his own people to do our work. An unoriginal plan you might think but the alternative that we allow the operation the Provisional's are planning to run its course and seek to intervene at the eleventh hour. The weakness of this is there is every likelihood they will change a component of the strategy. Ministerial guidance is requiring a more robust approach but I am persuaded by putting up Devlin- a shrewd operator but not top drawer. Your thoughts gentlemen?'

The country vicar had finished his notices and awaited the offering's. The silence remained un-interrupted for fully six minutes, save for an errant elbow on a cup and saucer. The clarity of the proposal with its tiered level of duplicity was matched paradoxically by the acute unease of virtually all those present. As the tension lingered, so did the pointed criticism of the political collusion.

'Is this not Murder by any other name? It won't end simply with Devlin. His cohorts will also be implicated and we run this risk of creating internal dissent within the republican ranks with the inherent risk of not only escalating feuds but the terrorist activity will become more random, more frenetic and more extreme. The more they lose control, so do we?' The Londonderry commander spoke with a quiet Scottish accent that sat outside the baritone Public schooled deliverance that was evident elsewhere. Advocates of the straightforward interventionist, arrest and detention approach were met with the repeated mantra of allowing at least one bird to be killed with one stone. The question of whether the commanding officer of Land Forces NI was aware of the proposals was met with an affirmative but the point was made by Sir that the plan needed consensus. Failure to agree, whilst it would be viewed as being regrettable, would require the reversion to more conventional measures. Those present reframed these remarks as a threat with Sir having a clear route to the top and who in turn will advise who was or wasn't in favour. Gossip which would halt a career march in its track. The combination of ethic's, vested interest and professional choice was an unwelcomed alliance, for some at least. Sir concluded with a further summary that skillfully push those assembled further into a corner, even if it was a well lit one.

'My role here is merely to put the options upon which the intelligence data is foundered. Devlin and his cell are planning something substantial and clearly it needs to be halted. The proposed course of action is a departure from usual policy but it does have I might add the honourable notion of preventing further mayhem. The anticipated trade off of putting up Devlin for dispatch is that we can use the splits, the recriminations and the subsequent disorganisation to our advantage and not as has been suggested which sound's more like a rather feeble apology for not doing a great deal just in case someone gets hurt.'

The Londonderry voice curbed his instinct to challenged but felt his view had been misrepresented and also knew his next posting was likely to involve visiting schools or overseeing catering arrangements at the staff college. Tacit unease abounded but acquiescence was implied in the silence. The details were put in place and a breakfast was taken in the knowledge that the tactics of warfare had departed from the requirements set down in Geneva but if it yielded results, so be it.

Pearson couldn't help but reflect on the impact that the proposed plan had caused such experienced soldiers. Their reaction could be touched. Means justifying the ends, the struggle of morality over pragmatism? What does that make me or of any of us, he thought. As each of the cars eased slowly away, the usual calm descended and the quiet sense of order was quickly re-established. Unbeknown to Pearson at this point was the wider impact that this plan was to have. What followed in the hours was to write a powerful script for the remainder of his life, defining how he felt and lived.

Chapter: 10

Tea was produced, unannounced, as Jacks took the mood and said very little. Pearson was looking pensive, more so as he reached for the sugar and stirred anti-clockwise,' for luck'. The nature of the briefing, a need to know, did not allow for a proper conversation. Each in their own way found this element of life strangely discomforting. They would share food but the bread breaking was left to others. Jacks only reference to the prevailing absence of dialogue indicated that all those who left were as equally troubled, perhaps more so. Both were on twilight, the late shift that took in sunset as well as the rise, non-existent at this time of the year. Pearson hated it, Jacks the opposite but they arrived at an accommodation, curbing each other's instincts to be, in turn, surly and animated. Some hours had past since the morning briefing but its legacy was in the room. They talked, a little about the news at home, about their respective lack of letters from friends and whether the discontented winter has now become an angry spring. They drifted into an inconclusive conversation about abstract thoughts. Pearson, putting the convention of rank aside as usual, fleetingly wondered why youngish men like him and

Jacks even bothered about such elements of thought. If it didn't matter, why did they not talk about rugby or cars, women or house prices? They concluded it was the mood which dictated their communication mode. Inevitably, the morning's briefing surfaced, having already been alluded to in different ways.

'It's at times like this that I feel little pride or value in our work or in the uniform.' This was an unexpected reference by Pearson to how he was feeling. Jacks, by not responding allowed space for the sentiment to be developed. And so it proved.

'You put countless hours into a briefing, summarising the anticipated deeds of others in the expectation that at best it will influence the action of others and in particular, their judgement. Instead, they are to gamble or juggle five different variables coming together with a view to exposing him.' Jacks knew immediately he was talking about Devlin, given he was central to the movement paths on his infamous chart.

'Consequently, rather than to allow the legal process to takes its course, we are all to collude with a more summary justice form.' Pearson flicked a glance at Jacks who was listening intensely. He provided an unsolicited response.

'As I see it, intelligence gathering is philosophy at work. It has no residual benefit or value unless it influences the process of decision making. It is about applying thought to an activity which in turn allows the balance of probabilities to determine themselves. In our case whatever happens to our opponents it feels almost preordained as is the case with this morning's meeting. The decision was almost certainly an 'au fait acompli', in other words, the routine of intelligence gathering was applied in its purest sense. I have seen this a great deal and put it down to how we think. It's structural. Debate is minimal. That's why I often feel that the activity of intelligence gathering is, in an absolute sense, facile. Our belief system requires us to have evidence before judgement is made. Often we act before all factors are known and understood but which I think is because the absolutists want certainty and we both know; it doesn't exist. Most of what we do is in itself facile but it has created a belief system that creates the perception of objectivity. This morning bears little relationship to rational thought. If Devlin is ghosted in some-way, the net impact could be far worse than any of us could imagine.'

All delivered without a trace of cynicism or glee. And this from a corporal, Pearson thought, somewhat embarrassed that he had subscribed to the rank rather than the ideal. Pearson found himself staring at Jacks observing his slight features and thin jaw line, his gaunt upper face and slight neck. As he talked, each part of the head complimented the other. The greater the intensity, the authority improved. He hadn't finished.

'Weber wrote at great length about constructs-'Construct Theory', god what a brain. He advanced the view that all things upon which humans design and place a value, in respect of the controlling elements which create order-governments, laws, economies and so on- are predicated on the belief that control must be at the centre. It is only within these parameters that freedom can exist. He wrote forever on the subject,' A fact about which Pearson accepted, unconditionally.

'Implicit in his argument is that all structures will yield difficulties irrespective of their intended purpose. The Justice system will create injustice, for example. Ulster is a construct, imposed on a sovereign nation state. Irrespective of the political motives or reasons why, it was constructed through the simple process of division. The rational was floored like most politically driven decisions as it took little or no account of local cultures or stabilising influences. Belfast, the surrounding districts and beyond have always been mixed as the populace have shared common purpose. Imposed governance: the worse form of democracy. And from London, ignoring the protestant merchants, or the catholic farmers and ship-yard workers and the power of the church. The imposition has constructed the perception of economic difference rather than one which has emerged. You can cope with the latter but not the former. If you create an artificial power base as with loyalists, they will seek to exploit it. Which they have for over fifty years. Should I shut up?'

Pearson followed the thesis and felt inclined to continue the discussion. Odd in the circumstances, as they both allowed their weight to be absorbed against a wall, standing by a sink.

'And you actually believe that by definition, all constructs are negative?'

'No. Simply that they create the potential for negativity and an abuse of power, like we have here. Whilst the various activities we try and stop are not justifiable, they are understandable, no matter how horrific.'

The quietness denoted that Jacks had moved into the personal with his last statement although Pearson did not need to draw attention to it. More tea managed to draw a line under a curious, un-self conscious discussion until the paper chase started again. The early morning hand-over provided Pearson time for a shower followed by a deep sleep. Unbeknown to either of them, this was the last conversation they were to ever have.

*

The speed and intensity of the wind was sufficient in its sustained, trembling burst's to have woken Pearson. He lay, motionless, holding the palm of his left hand behind the part of the head mirrors never reveal. The sleep had done little to remove that feeling of not being right from deep below his rib cage. The mood took him back to London, to a school without learning and an area dominated by variety. He visualised several friends, too many no doubt, rootless and having never achieved. His parents earnestly believing that Sunday school for a youngster represented something. Scouts, no TV, with time spent not being allowed out, and lots of talk about not getting on. He twisted and stretched for his watch. At the point he was fully extended, a rasping knock on the door caused him to jump, almost in fear such was the noise. The base was a place where sudden, harsh sounds were rare hence his start and momentary loss of concentration. The voice that followed the knock did not match its harshness. It was muted, apologetic and somewhat stuttering. Initially, Pearson was unable to make out who it was until the Scottish lilt resonated as belonging to Corporal Money, Gladwyn's man. Incongruously, a note was slipped under the door written upon which was a simple statement, saying to be with 'Sir' within Three minutes. The words 'It's serious' put in brackets, merely added to the small piece of melodrama: for Pearson to have been summoned like this and for it not to be serious would have been unlikely. It was almost 13.00hrs.

Pearson entered the room, noting that the moment the door handle had moved back into position, the four men present immediately stood up. Gladwyn and Sir each flanked by a military policeman, lower in rank but higher in gravitas than others. Formally addressing his Senior Officers, 'Sir' cut through Pearsons drift into the expected protocol.

'Thank you for coming at such short notice. I'll get to the point of your deliverance here momentarily. Perhaps we might all sit.'

Gladwyn looked unkempt and stared intensely at Pearson, his face was that of someone suppressing a rage, a personal torment about which clearly all others new something. Gladwyn could barely sit within his own skin.

'Can I first introduce you to Sergeant Musto and Sergeant Spring? There presence here, by definition, denotes something of great importance.' The pause was that of an executioner before the axe fell. The passive calm engendered by Sir was neither matched nor appreciated by the others. Their eyes indicated the bestowing of terror.

'Corporal Jacks has left the base without authority. His whereabouts are unknown as are the reasons or the circumstances of his going. It became evident earlier this afternoon when I required him to clarify an aspect at the mapping we had of BCC. Within about Ten Minutes, it became evident he was elsewhere. This position is grave and I am most perplexed by what has happened.'

The words drifted round Person, smearing him as each sentence linked with the previous one. Anything was believable but not this. A mistake, a joke, a prank perhaps. Yet, as each crushing blow of the axe fell, the initial indifference of his senior officer became less endearing with voice tone embracing a menacing timbre allied with a climate akin to a screeching blackboard, or a motorway without lights, in a fog.

'Major Gladwyn has a few questions, if you would be so kind.'

He held the pause long enough and with it, affected a languid air of the bully. His opening remarks were accusatory and ill defined which Pearson found strangely out of character but he put his responses without the need for anything other than receiving thoughts, ideas and even the truth.

'You were the last person to have spoken with Jacks. What frame of mind was he in?'

'You are making an assumption about me being the last person. I went to bed soon after the detail had finished. I couldn't be absolutely sure that he went directly to his room or indeed elsewhere.'

'Well he's clearly gone elsewhere, hasn't he and as for your reference to making assumptions, I am entitled to make a few, am I not, given he was your man who is now missing am I not, Lieutenant Pearson. Well, am I?'

He was not going to allow this line, irrespective of the risks. It is I who is being accused, the conspirator, he thought. Pearson caught sight of Musto's sudden movement that denoted a degree of uncertainty about where Gladwyn was taking this dialogue. He gambled with his next response.

'Captain Gladwyn; You can of course make assumptions about anything you like but please ensure they are just that.

It is neither a fact or in any way evidential that I was the last person to see him. Correct me if I am wrong but the timescales involved here would indicate he has exited the base in daylight. I did speak with him around 8.30am but not afterwards. As we were on twilight shift, I turned in, especially after the morning briefing that was held. We both know he could have spoken to various different individuals afterwards. I trust you take my point, Sir.'

Pearson waited for the response from Gladwyn, which at the point of its arrival, was delivered at too greater speed for 'Sir' who asked him to both check his language and talk more slowly. He went on.

'You make what is a small but bogus point about what you pompously refer to as my assumption. The whole base knows that you and Jacks would always talk at the end of each shift. It was a feature of your relationship, wasn't it?'

'I am puzzled as to how you can speak for the whole base, Sir. Implicit in what you are saying is that I know something of Jacks movement or apparent disappearance. Perhaps that should be your starting point.'

This comment was fraught with danger for Pearson, defining how the dialogue was to be controlled. He had introduced the notion or suggestion that he knew something about Jacks. By introducing it, irrespective of the reasons or motives, changed the emphasis, so moving the focus on him and away from Jacks or the prevailing circumstances.

'Pearson, I think we both can agree that those remarks are best shelved. Captain Gladwyn is merely asking you some questions: routine given what has occurred. You along with everyone else present must recognise that once word spreads, this whole community will be awash with rumour and anxiety. That will extend beyond here with confidence being damaged to the point of no return. Is it best therefore if I ask you the direct question, simply; do you have any knowledge or insight into where Jacks might be or his motives for leaving?'

'I have no idea, Sir, none whatsoever. I am as shocked as your-self. Someone must have seen him leave. The Guard duty detail for one.'

'That is to be established, hence our colleagues from Police personnel. They will do all the necessary scrutiny checks but as yet, the Guard house is not aware of the situation. Information management is critical. At this point it is only us who are aware of the situation. Hardly the chosen few but a critical mass nonetheless. All I can add at this point is that it is likely he exited under dusk cover but quite how is to be determined. Perhaps it is best you return to your quarters and allow the situation to become clearer. Rule seven applies as you would expect.'

A moment elapsed before the enormity found its way in. As he thawed and so began to move, he resisted the urge to pose some of the more obvious questions with a security bias. Who opened the gate, what is the camera saying, was a bike involved? If so, was it seen or heard? Nothing was clear other than the suppressed rage within, directed at Gladwyn who had already convicted his version of the guilty.

Pearson sat staring; each movement accentuated the quietness that he felt, matching a mood that combined fear with practical curiosity. Relaxed, given he had no sense or understanding about what had happened although a less tolerant emotion would surface when he considered the tone of questioning. Working through the scenario, he posed the question; to do what? Motives and conclusions would be arrived at once the detail emerged. The first; he had lost his sense of judgement and perspective and so had run. Retaining ones nerve was always overrated. Or secondly; he had been turned, gone 'double'. A more unlikely scenario Pearson could not imagine. He dismissed both thoughts quickly, choosing to pass the benefit of any doubt to the essentially uncomplicated and dedicated soldier. His thoughts began turning towards home, and his parents. His father was, apparently, very much like Jacks. Talkative, focussed on the task in hand. Something of a thinker but with the intellectual rigour demanded of a secondary modern pupil. A dedicated gatherer of trivia, mainly sporting that would be used to break the mood. Essentially, both were company people, neither retaining a shred of malice.

An hour passed. Rule seven having been invoked meant that he was forbidden to leave his quarter or talk to anyone unless in the presence of a Senior Officer. He sensed the tension from his window. Two more unmarked cars had arrived out of which stepped various military people, a mixture of police and security personnel. He attempted to read, watched a short programme for Open University students, on the poet, Gerald Manley-Hopkins. He ironed two shirts within a climate of growing anticipation that his next meeting and discussion with the base commander was likely to be predicated on blame and would take the form of a controlled interrogation. Reason, objectivity and any attempted understanding would be secondary. And so it proved. He was given a ten minute standby call, to be presented again to Sir, Gladwyn and others. Perhaps some news would be forthcoming. It was all a mistake. An error. He would appear and shout; 'April fool'.

As he entered the room, he was transported back a generation into a world in which he never quite fitted. He wrestled with the inner sense of seeking approval from those to whom outwardly at least, he needed to show deference. He did not find a great deal of comfort, however. He sensed this was the gathering of a shooting party such was the unspoken aggression. Eye contact was lost on those present as they sought to usher him into place, both physical as well as emotionally. Perhaps they had forgotten the eight days in the boot of a car in West Belfast which had equipped him with an inner resolve that few uniforms and even fewer suits had ever remotely experienced. The somewhat feeble attempt at intimidation therefore had seemed strangely misplaced. To have breathed through only one nostril in order to minimize or eliminate noise or else face immediate death invited the understanding of fear. Words, even if harsh, without the presence of death was easy to manage by comparison although perhaps this scenario would pose different questions. Gladwyn looked frozen with uncertainty, with the base commander having seemingly aged Ten years, looking resigned. The military policemen had been replaced by RUC police liaison and a woman who was not introduced other than by a euphemistic title of observer.

Sir made an initial point that he wished to create an air of business like informality to discuss what was clearly a difficulty. Pearson immediately felt less at ease, having categorised this statement in the ' this will hurt me more...' group. The absurdity was merely added to. A former classroom in which singing and play was the norm had been supplanted by or replaced with malevonance.

'Points needed to be clarified, questioned asked, assurances sought. That sought of thing. The questioning was likely to go on for a time so you must ask for a break when required. It will help us all if from the outset, you are clear Lieutenant Pearson.' Sir could not or was not prepared to hide his perceptible unease, as the words left a mouth that was beyond tense. His lips were unable to move yet the term truthful was clearly on his lips also but that was held back in reserve. Sir rambled on, uncharacteristically diffident and uncertain, constantly repeating various simple points of procedure, all of which added to the perspective of controlled farce.

'This isn't an interrogation or a court of enquiry you understand, if that helps.' It would if he knew what he meant but he remained silent. The observer was evidently disquieted by this remark as the discolouration of her neck revealed. Her left arm also became restless.

The questioning proceeded at a measured pace. Pearson's career profile and background were picked over. Little was challenged or dwelt upon. Historical performance reports of two years ago were revisited in a manner that seemed functional and without interest. His arrival at the base, his recruitment notes, induction and probationary period were referred to as was his initial dealing with Gladwyn. His transition through to being fully operational was highlighted as being unproblematic with every indication that he was proving to be a strong influence on his team and a person who liked order. Jacks at this point had not been mentioned or even acknowledged until unexpectedly his named figured. Sir introduced him as possessing 'doubtful sexuality.' Pearson's riposte engendered a note of relief when Jacks was again referred to as someone 'less than natural.'

'We shared many things both in deed and word but any hand holding was merely metaphysical. In any event, Corporal Jacks was in no way Homosexual- even here.'

The observer twitched as the left side of her mouth moved slightly upwards. Sir droned on, moving through Jacks' career, summarising the type of relationship expected between ranks held by Jacks and Pearson. It was described as pivotal. 'Eyes and ears, hearts and minds- that sought of thing.' He was, is, in every-way, a top performer for which Pearson can take his share of credit, particularly when dealing with recent data. Which makes this whole business so utterly worrying', remark's spat out with no regard for those present.

The quietness passed. Pearson recognised that the discursive nature by way of introduction was a prelude to, no doubt, a more rigorous form of linked statements. He was genuinely puzzled by his indifference to this element of the process. And yet, as each minute passed, the realization that he was in some way caught up in something about which he had no control or influence descended. He was also surprised by his own response towards Jacks departure. As he sat there, he concluded that he wasn't shocked as he had already concluded that whatever Jacks had done, he would have been in control of his motives and movement. This conclusion however, was to change within the next hour or so. The question of why was supplanted by when and for what purpose. There would be a purpose.

Gladwyn took centre stage. He looked unkempt and edgy but no matter how hard he attempted to affect an image of gravity, he failed. His anger got in the way, causing him to appear more like a lofty prefect than an inquisitor. He dug around Jacks' strengths and weaknesses, commenting that for a corporal, he was remarkably well read. This was a waspish remark that seemed out of context for the hearing. He pursued the theme, however, which allowed Pearson to change the emphasis. Gladwyn was floundering in personalised invective, causing his questioning to miss there mark.

'Lieutenant Pearson; How would you characterised your relationship with Jacks?'

'That of a good colleague, subordinate in rank, someone who deferred to this status. He was totally loyal, utterly reliable, thorough, an authority on the street politics of Belfast and beyond, amusing company and without a trace of envy. He was resigned to moving on later this year and was preparing for his next promotion board. He felt that he possessed certain characteristics that might detract from his credentials as a sergeant and they needed addressing.'

'Would you like to describe these ''characteristics'' he had'?

'I said they were how he describes himself not as I saw them.'

'So, second guess him.'

'Essentially, he is a shy man, lacking part of his personality that was outgoing or direct. He saw this as a disadvantage. He also said that he had never met a sergeant who wore glasses or who was short. These comments represented a view of himself that didn't quite fit or accord with his perception of what was required to achieve promotion. In a self deprecating way, he viewed himself as a follower. He regretted not spending more time in operational posts. He said he felt this would have given him an edge.'

'Is that it?' Gladwyn was staring but not listening.

'Yes. I think it is. What he couldn't see was that his innate intelligence and thoughtfulness also had its place within the forces. As we all know, we are surrounded by individuals who lead first and think second.'

This remark induced a half-smile from 'sir' and the observer but seemed to pass Gladwyn by.

'Has anything changed within the past few hours caused you to reflect on anything you have said or at least reconsider?'

'No. Not at all.'

'Lieutenant Pearson, I find that statement utterly remarkable. Corporal Jacks has left this base without any authority whatsoever and yet you still view him as some worthy, principled individual with whom you felt able to offer some misplaced career counselling?'

He didn't answer; a response that clearly annoyed Gladwyn who persisted in layering each question in a more accusatory tone. He was seeking to discredit the Junior Officer as well as making him look slight and without depth. Before he entered the room, Pearson had already taken in the enormity of the situation and made some internal judgements about how far the anticipated smearing would be allowed to reach. He quickly concluded that there were some more words to exchange but he sensed that the others present were not with him. As Gladwyn persisted, each word seemed to remove a stitch from the epilates which denoted his commission and which in all probability would end his military career.

'Lieutenant Pearson, your response to my questioning and that of the Senior Officers has at best been largely neutral and certainly do not convey any sense that you appreciate what has occurred. At worst, you convey indifference and discourtesy to this panel. For the last time, I want you to explain to those of us who have a vested interest in knowing, what on earth you feel has gone on? You are the man's lead Officer and by your own admission are both close to him and knowledgeable about his habits and moods and even his motives, it would seem. And now he has vanished. Why?'

Pearson sought an alliance with at least one other in the room but the relationship, or a connection wasn't evident. They either looked at Gladwyn or at their notes.

'The only response I can give you is this: if Corporal Jacks left this base, he would have done so having obeyed an order.' Like a tracer bullet, this response was delivered as a statement of intent to Gladwyn who reacted as though he hadn't quite heard what was said. Sir reacted as if having been personally accused of a capital offence. His contained rage and indignation caused him to slur his initial response. In a previous era, he would have no doubt reached for his sword or at least cuffed the accuser with a gauntlet. The male suit sat deeper in his chair and the women observer quietly suggested that Gladwyn, by now on his feet ready to trade blows, sit down. Pearson was not surprised by the reaction but neither did he have a sense of if he was right. Not yet at least.

'You must either retract that remark or account for it at a commission of enquiry that will undoubtedly result in your Court Martial. You do, I'm sure appreciate the enormity of what you are suggesting?'

Sir had shed his countryman demeanour and had acquired the aura of the interrogator he once was, seeking the essence, the smell of what was being alleged.

'Answer now', Gladwyn rasped, distressed and almost child-like in his manner. The smearing must now end, thought Pearson, as he attempted to piece together a response worthy of the moment.

'Let's be clear about what is in this room, now, as we discuss this episode. What is present is so transparently obvious that I feel insulted. Implied in every facet of this process is that I, in someway, know of Jacks' whereabouts or his motives for leaving this unit. I don't and I too am as shocked and surprised as each of you here. What is also in this domain is that I am not being heard or believed which in the circumstances is initially at least understandable but it has persisted. There has been a whole series of unspoken transactions going on that I am in some-way implicated or even responsible for his departure. What has not been said but clearly alluded to is that his disappearance has coincided with a major intelligence episode about to be actioned. Is he implicated? Well, I for one do not know. What I do know is that one gets a sense of the values and instincts of a person when in their command. Jacks is the consummate army man. If he left this base it was because he was being asked to do something-obeying an order. For him to leave without authority would be unthinkable. Unless, of course I have seriously misread him, his work and his moral position.'

'Which given your performance and lack of substance or insight to date is highly probable, is it not Pearson?'

'I think that remark says more about you Captain Gladwyn than anything else you have insinuated previously. Whilst recognising that you are the senior officer in this dialogue, I resent your personalisation of this issue and I believe it is a wise to call a short recess before you end up making a complete fool of yourself. You are an embarrassment.'

Gladwyn's anger was less dramatic but more intense as he attempted to remind Pearson of his rank and wanted to immediately initiate putting him on a charge. In light of what he said, his remedy was a fatuous statement of the obvious, uttered by someone bereft of power and so could only resort to his status in order to regain the authority that had already left. The commander again intervened.

'I am inclined to agree with Pearson's request and will permit a short recess of Thirty minutes. When you return, Lieutenant Pearson, you will be asked to account for several things that you have said and hopefully in a manner in keeping with your rank as an officer and not of some street fighter seeking to mask the truth. The questions posed by Captain Gladwyn were entirely consistent with the legitimate pursuit of information about Jacks. Your response to them merely compounded the suspicion that you know more than you are saying. If that isn't the case then provide a more measured response in order to explain yourself.'

'Sir; perhaps during this recess your panel can reconsider its strategy of questioning given the way I have been simply accused. I would have expected better from yourself and Captain Gladwyn- you are after-all my superior Officers.'

'The accusatory tone as you put it does have a context does it not?'

'The context should take into account the circumstances and not simply make a connection between myself, Jacks and his disappearance. I will not withdraw my view that I think he would be obeying an order. Without any sense of self doubt I think this to be the case. What I know is that I never gave it.'

With the quiet ushering of chairs, Pearson left, sat in his room and realised that he had indeed ended his military career in a way that he could not have imagined.

*

Ruth was mesmerised as Pearson, like peeling an onion, moved each layer in an attempt to reach the centre, the core. She so wanted to interject but the monotone of the narrator did not allow for or invite comment. He simply needed to talk and she allowed him. By now, they had moved to her lounge, positioned to allow space in which the words could enter and be understood and to be quietly edited to create the natural order of the story. He hadn't finished and for differing reasons, their sensitivities were aroused to the point that the lateness of the hour was ignored. Its conclusion was needed.

Chapter: 11

A feature of the past few hours had been the number of times the door of Pearson's quarter had been knocked. This occasion, the drum beat was quiet, more refined with longer gaps between the gentle tap-tapping. He was caught by surprise when, on opening, he found the observer standing with her back towards him.

'Can I help you, mam? I'm not entirely sure if I am allowed to talk to you as I am under special measures.'

'Can I come in?'

'That is not allowed and I assume you know that.'

'The commander is aware of my visit and it is permissible.'

Ill at ease at presenting with an air of disbelief as well as sadness, he stepped aside, gestured for her to sit down and as she did, he joined her. She looked calm, if a little cold, preferring to keep her large trench-coat on with her hands thrust deep into her pocket as she stared at the young man, some years her junior. Neither spoke for what seemed like an age until she enquired if he was OK and was prepared to answer some questions away from the glare of his immediate colleagues.

When he asked why, she acknowledged the pressure everyone was under so maybe it would help if they simply talked. Pearson concluded that this was probably some attempt to soften him up and to adopt a different tactic, poorly thought through, almost certainly by Gladwyn.

'I would prefer not to say anything to anyone unless someone else was present. Besides, you were introduced to me as observer- of the process- rather than a contributor. So no, I do not wish to talk with you but thank you for your concern.'

Somewhat taken aback by the consistency of his manner, she made a reference to the fact that she was there to help, he had nothing to fear but clearly there were issues that needed to be talked through.

'Not for me there wasn't. Without wishing to appear disrespectful, your presence here is making feel uncomfortable.'

'At least allow me to make some observations then, otherwise this whole mess might move into the realms of some uncontrolled witch-hunt that will serve little purpose.'

'You're here, as you say, with the permission of others so I have little say in what you want to comment on but I am not saying anything and I'm most certainly not looking to detract from anything I've said.'

He wanted to believe she was an ally, the critical friend, the believer in him. It never worked like that of course. The labyrinth of players within the security world created its own illusions. Enemies became friends, friends became informants, and informants became superior officers. Along the way, the truth becomes corrupted with a constant state of uncertainty and caution being evident. A trainer back at Cirencester quoted every day the Russian maxim of 'assume nothing'. Pearson was to apply this rigorously given the present scene. But still he wanted to believe in the observer. Open faced, worldly, the possessor of a marriage ring, understated perfume that permeated the otherwise dank atmosphere of the centre.

How welcomed such a smell was. Her suit suggested an expensive, non civil service choice of fabric that added to her sense of stabilised charm. As a consequence, she began to exude an inner confidence in dealing with this situation which curiously, did not make Pearson feel any easier. She persisted.

'Let us first assume that you are telling the truth. If Jacks left the base, you are of the view that he would have done so having responded to an order as opposed to going on some other pretext. Are you prepared to say anything else about who do you think gave the order and for what purpose?'

'As I've already stated, I am not prepared to say anything else.'

'If you are lying then you have a vested interest in presenting that scenario to the panel in order to detract from the obvious view that it was you who gave Jacks authority to leave.'

'I have no authority to issue any such command. All the junior ranks are aware of that so they wouldn't even ask. On the rare occasions it has happened, a request is made and granted for someone to leave, it really is quite an issue to administer. The authority is vested with the base commander. No one else unless it has been formally delegated via the Commander of Land Forces to the Two IC, in this case Captain Gladwyn. It is that bigger deal. But the time scales do not hang together. All this is very evident and I've already said as much to the panel earlier. I also made the point that Jacks could have simply left without any authority but there appeared to be little presenting evidence for this. And of course it isn't easy to leave here, as you know. How does anyone walk out during early morning daylight?'

It again went quiet. Pearson, looking pensive but in control, sought eye contact that was met although it suggested other concerns. Preoccupation with something extra was a feature of all security personnel, especially at times like this. She left the room, neatly clipping the door only for it to open in a less controlled interruption to remind him that he will be summoned again in a few moments for more questioning. He resisted the urge to retort that he was reluctant to cooperate as this would be viewed as antagonistic but that was his instinct. He also resisted any further analysis of what had happened. He reminded himself of the last image his corporal had portrayed and the routine indifference their last encounter had generated. The speed at which this had changed, his virtual house arrest and the prevailing sense of tension detracted from his inner sense of order but not to the degree that he had assumed. He chose to sit on the floor to await the summons which, when it arrived, he decided to be even more belligerent.

In fact, several hours passed before any further contact was made, so allowing for some sleep, a shower and some reading. The short, assertive knock followed the announcement of his name, interrupted the calmness. It was Gladwyn, sounding tired but retained enough sentiment in his voice to denote the sustained rage. Five minutes were permitted to allow a collecting of thoughts before he was again taken to Sirs office, to be greeted by the same group as previously. Coffee was offered but declined, so indicating a change in mood which was unexpected but suspect.

'The news is bleak I'm afraid so prepare yourself. We have received word that Corporal Jacks has been found dead. Early reports suggest that he had been shot, executed more like, with his body being found about Twelve miles from here, half-naked, trussed and hooded. You will of course be very shocked so I would advise caution before you say anything. Allow yourself time to absorb the news, is what I'm saying. As I speak, there is an investigation going on naturally but we are not releasing any details until a clearer picture emerges of why he left here. Suffice it to say his family will be told within the next few hours but we need to be selective about what is said. You might want to say something and I will then outline what I am proposing to do next.'

Curiously, Pearson's initial thoughts concentrated on the timescales. Almost Twenty Four hours had passed that had seen Jacks leave the base and then murdered. Fast by anyone's standard. Then a grey mist descended, one that was associated with an overwhelming sense of sadness and disbelief. Rapid, connected thoughts were moving around his upper body whilst his legs felt numb and in some-way, unrelated to his being. His belongings, his parents, and his capacity to brew tea: Pearson would deal with these things when time had elapsed. The fleeting image of his semi-nakedness, hands tied, unable to resist. He sat on his own hands so eliciting an intuitive sense of concern from the observer who had already concluded that Pearson had little to add to proceedings. Quietly spoken, Pearson asked if he would be allowed to be the appointed liaison officer for the family. It was felt to be too early to decide that but it was unlikely. Anymore details about Jacks death were deemed to be beyond Pearson's province and so regretfully little more would be added. Jacks room had already been cleared which fitted with a reference by Sir that suggested he had 'never worked here.' Any application by base personnel to attend any funeral was out of the question and would be blocked. 'Business as usual, for some at least.' Sir was abrupt, agitated and without warmth. He also was unable to sustain eye contact.

'Which brings us neatly backed to you Lieutenant Pearson. Of course you will be upset by the news but one wonders if you are altogether surprised. Be that as it may. As for now, you are to be taken into military custody for further questioning. Your tour here has effectively ended but clearly there remains a whole series of unanswered questions which you need to resolve in the proper way. This panel remains wholly and unequivocally unconvinced with your stance to date, not helped by you declining all attempts of responding to the reasonable questioning and prompts to establish your involvement in this whole business. Arrangements are being made to have you collected.'

Pearson knew it was facile to react other than to make reference to those present that his needs were insignificant to those of Jacks' family and he hoped they would be treated with a dignity that was lacking over the past few hours. He was asked to explain that remark but refused.

'Little else I have said to date has been heard or acknowledged so I won't waste my breath. Am I being arrested or merely invited to go quietly into custody?'

'The latter. You will not be permitted to return to your quarter. As you leave this room, you will voluntarily submit yourself to colleagues outside this door and taken off. Thereafter, it is out of my hands. Dismissed.'

As he stood up, he stared intently at the observor, seeking a moment's recognition of the abuse of process but none was forthcoming. The wryest of smile covered his otherwise expressionless face, resigned to the fact that for now, this life was over.

*

'I have a need to keep talking, to keep explaining. I hope it isn't dull. This is very important for me.' Ruth stared at the lined face, now more complete than the many years before and edged nearer to him. An arm stretched and brushed an imaginary hair from a marked cheek and held the hand against his ear. She said nothing, but stared with an intensity that said everything about her interest. He again continued.

Chapter: 12

The Military Policemen, of which there were two, unusually in plain clothes, were polite and respectful of his rank. They explained that they were driving north into Belfast and he was to be questioned firstly at the Barracks near Newtownards and thereafter, flown back to the mainland and depending on the outcome, either held at Colchester or returned to his base in Aldershot. They seemed uncomplicated men, the likes of which Pearson had worked with during the past two or so years, many times. They made it clear that they were not permitted to talk although they did allude to the fact that they were aware of developments at the base. Pearson looked intently from the window, catching signs of spring and the apparent lack of traffic as they approached the city. Radio contact was established with his destination. Time of arrival was Four minutes with a request for open access on entry. A code was offered and accepted and he assumed the term 'quarry passive' referred to him. An image of Jacks had stayed with him ever since he was told of his fate and he found himself equating the irony of the trouble his friend had caused. The irony was giving way to the image of his friend, bereft of his spectacles and virtually all his clothes and seemingly more than half-naked, being shot then discarded and so joining other service personnel of a current and past age; being executed without a trial. What on earth had he done to deserve that? Death was intruding into Pearson's consciousness. Through a checkpoint, left, acceleration then a rather harsh sequence of braking ended a journey of some forty-five minutes. He was asked to remain seated until some minor formalities were completed which seemed reasonable if unexpected. Eventually he was shown into an 'induction' suite, allowed to use the bathroom, offered some refreshments and then seated in a room. He made a feeble joke to himself that it wasn't form to be beaten up on an empty stomach or a full bladder. Jacks again intruded on his thinking that changed his mood although this was interrupted by an entry of a stern looking non-uniformed male and the reappearance of the observer.

'I believe you have already met my colleague Janet Peel.'

Eye contact at last although her attempt at hand shaking was incongruous and out of place so wasn't met. Pearson looked at her and detected less certainty in her manner than previously and he was determined not to do anything that was to alleviate her particular, obvious suffering.

'My name is Robert Chisholm. We are both from military intelligence although we are duty bound to inform you that if we feel there is presenting evidence of any criminal wrongdoing, we pass such matters to the RUC. To get to the piece as speedily as we can, you are under suspicion of facilitating the departure of Corporal Jacks from the base where you were both deployed. The subsequent discovery of his body and the circumstances of his death had aroused various issues of concern that will necessitate some fairly robust answers. At its simplest, the suggestion is that you were aware of his intended exit from the base as his controlling officer but did nothing to intervene, so suggesting a degree of collusion and duplicity culminating in duty avoidance and subsequent dereliction. Chances are, you have worked out all this before your arrival here but the finger is well and truly pointing at you. Your conduct during questioning at the base was described as evasive, lacking in authority or understanding and on three occasions you were overtly insubordinate to Captain Gladwyn. Moving you from the base was a pre-requisite I'm afraid and you will not be returning. Our line of questioning will be self-evidently direct and the time is now, so to speak, to get honest. We have received a briefing from your commander who was fairly scathing about you although his remarks paled into insignificance to what Gladwyn has said. Even allowing for the emotion of the situation, it doesn't help you much. Hence the reason for the need to get the whole business done and dusted. What I want to say is that I'm familiar with your service record, having read your papers and it is apparent to me that it speaks for itself. So, if you have gone funny, talk on the understanding that we will try and work something out. Hopefully you appreciate our candour.'

A technique he was taught at Cirencester was to cite some basic numerical rhythms to himself; phone numbers, line-out calls, Cricket score's. The purpose being to clear his mind from the usual and understandable position of wanting to talk or shout. Confess, deny, question- all pointless responses at the time when his inquisitor was likely to be full of anxiety and no little concern about his own performance. Say nothing but look interested, perhaps even calm but say nothing. Sit with the silence for longer than was imaginable, and then speak. More numbers. He did this and by doing so, moved the axis of inter-personal authority if not the actual power that sat in the room.

'I've not heard your colleague speak yet. You will know from my record Mr Chisholme that I neither want or expect others to do anything except talk for themselves so I would like to hear from Miss. Peel given our last encounter was predicated on her departing from the rules and I'm not an idiot.'

Chisholm found these references obscure. Looking at his colleague, he invited her to offer similar reassurances but already, the inquisitors were mindful that this encounter was hardly going to follow the usual process. Her neck coloured. The room was equipped with the standard public sector items of utility. A table, no windows, four of the ubiquitous inverted 'question mark' wooden chairs, no pictures although a notice board contained a copy of the factories act, advising those who were interested to be aware of Health and Safety in the work place. Topical, Pearson thought. The room had a surprisingly fresh smell to it but it was a place that suggested little in terms of being welcoming.

'Am I allowed a legal representative to be present?'

'No, because you are not under caution or indeed arrest.'

'Am I allowed a fellow officer or indeed anyone else present?'

'Why would you want that?' Chisholm seemed genuinely perplexed. Miss Peel less so.

'Please answer the question.'

'No, not at this stage.'

'At what stage, then?'

'Not now, no'

Pearson allowed the pause in dialogue to hang, concluding at speed that neither of his apparent adversary's was clear about their role. Numbers.

'OK- can I have the interview taped then, as a record of the transaction? A post card'?

'Post card? No, that also isn't possible or necessary. Mr Pearson we need to get moving and whilst I regret the fact I cannot be more helpful, that is how it is.'

'You cannot be more helpful. Well, Can Miss Peel assist? These are basic rules, enshrined in just about every procedure there is. Can you help mam? '

Her pause had a different feel to it. Clearly marginal to the process, the best she provided was a re-wording of what Mr Chisholm said.

'OK- all I would ask is that you appreciate that your names will feature in any future investigations as Two colleagues who felt unable to assist a member of the military who was being questioned in connection with what amounts to allegation of at best conspiracy or at worst, being an enemy agent. Emotive stuff and not a time to choose to ignore the rules as you have. I note also that neither of you appear to have any paper on which to take a note nor are showing any basic ID. What is this? What is the status of this meeting?'

Chisholm's voice lowered and affected an image of the absent friend, the all embracing confidant, offering assurances at every turn about the process, the need for everyone to be open, wanting to establish the facts and so forth. Believing not a word of it Pearson indicated that his trust in both the process and the processors was non-existent but he would gladly provide a summary of what he had already said before.

An hour, perhaps two, came and went as Pearson explained his version of events. He made repeated references to Jacks' general state, this being one of permanently and unfailingly unproblematic. He described their last encounter, after the main briefing and how they had talked at length before Pearson had adjourned to bed. He recited some hypothetical scenarios which might allow him to conclude Jacks was less than honest but offered countering evidence which did not add up to an indictment of him. Pearson said, more than once, that it would be easy for him to build a case against his man, to daub him with the air of uncertainty which was all that was needed to confirm suspicions. But he couldn't and what is more he had no basis. He concluded his extensive recital with a further reference to the belief that he was obeying an order. It was of course conceivable that he had left under his own accord but this image did not fit with Pearson's assessment.

'He left that base having followed an order. This goes to the heart of the issue and it is evident neither of you two or other's can comprehend that an order of exit was given and is not being owned with the resultant implication being that he was sent out on some dodgy pre-text to which neither the base commander or Gladwyn is prepared to acknowledge. What you are left with is the belief that I issued the order, which I didn't or couldn't, or he went under his own steam or he went having been given authority to. We keep coming back to the same theme. My work with Jacks and our relationship was professionally driven. He is now dead and what I have to face is a real cocktail of emotions having been accused of one thing whilst feeling something else. Fairness isn't at the top of your agenda but this whole process is floored and I suspect you sense that the linear nature of your plodding questions is actually missing some vital ingredients.'

'Which are?' Chisholm's reaction sounded genuine puzzled perhaps but no more, with these references.

'As part of your questioning, have you established whether I was the last person to speak to Jacks? The base is a very small, goldfish bowl of a place with any movement being both seen and heard. Jacks' was a restless sleeper, and he was always on the go. It would have been fairly unremarkable for personnel from other shifts seeing him around on their watch, making tea, just being around. Has either Gladwyn or Sir said anything about whether they saw him?'

'They said they didn't.'

'Well, I suppose I am bound to say they would say that but has it been verified or corroborated? When we left each other we were going to bed, simple as that. The fact that no one, and I mean no one saw him leave makes it's doubly suspicious. For anyone to leave that place and not be seen? We are talking Houdini type stuff. No, he's been allowed to leave based on an exit order- unheard of for quite sometime, if ever. If either of those Two are denying this then look deeper. I am not even saying that the exit order wasn't justified but Jacks had no reason to leave. He was sent.' Janet Peel almost spoke, opening her mouth and moving her right hand as if to gesture something of importance but then withdrew.

'They deny this and it has been accepted.'

'Well, you best charge me with something then because I have nothing left to add or say. I suspect you won't want to as we know you haven't a bean on me. I cannot disprove that I've helped Jacks over the fence, to carry out some major act of something anymore than you can prove it. If my name has been put up as a conspirator, fine; but produce the evidence and I will contest it. If there is some form of whispering campaign against me, with senior people suggesting I am in some way not enough or incomplete then so be it. Produce the names, produce the evidence, produce the detail but at least allow me the dignity of ending a career which creates some space between the facts and the fantasy. And at least allow me the inner belief that you two are being thorough, painstakingly rigorous in the wish that if you are going to stitch me up, at least do it professionally. Or if you are objective and working outside of the usual rules, do me the service of at least conceding I might have a point.' Pearson, by now tired but less challenging almost implored his next few sentences.

'Jacks did not leave that base without approval. Believe me. It wasn't in his nature to behave any differently. Given the reaction against me, I would look closer at my superior officers. So please: get on and charge me or at least do something.'

The initiative had been taken by Pearson and he knew it. Three, possibly four adjournments took place, with his inquisitors leaving the room at given times, to check details. The questioning moved, in not too a sophisticated way to his value base, how he viewed the republican cause; could he ever envisage a time when he might become a supporter of the struggle. Chisholm made several references to the injustice so many catholics felt and how it wasn't a surprise that the English were to get a bloody nose. Pearson's unguarded response to correct him by referring to the 'British' opened up a whole series of questions about the motive of this comment: it assuming an importance which they both found unconvincing but motions were gone through. An eventual break was called for with Pearson given the authority to sleep. When he was woken after about an hour, he was faced by a tired looking Chisholm holding some papers.

'This is what you are going to do. You will resign your commission with an agreed citation of your military career acknowledging your achievement whilst stating that due to personal circumstances you requested to be released from your posting. Your record will reflect the honourable nature of your discharge and you are assured that there will be no mention of this business. You will of course receive all your entitlements and you will be written to as per normal. The resignation will be accepted with immediate effect and as from now you will not be privy to any more discussions or indeed be questioned about the whole of the Jacks thing. In this regard that episode has now closed. Now before you say anything I want you to listen very closely to what I'm saying. If you make any attempt either now or in the future to make a claim against the Army or the MOD for unfair dismissal or any of that victim nonsense, your testimonial will change, your entitlements ended and in essence your future blighted. This is a small price to pay for the hole I've dug you out. The other side of this very odd coin is the fact that you are contaminated with the Jacks business. The perception is you know more than you are saying and out of some perverse loyalty to a junior rank you have said nothing. Whether that perception is fair or not, it exists and extends into high places. The disappointment that surrounds you is immense. The only reason I have brokered this deal is simply not being able to disprove you claims. That is due to the operational state of your detail where collecting evidence has been impossible. And yet if we find a shred of anything that you sent Jacks to his grave, you will be hounded. For what it's worth I haven't formed a view about you Pearson but something simply isn't right with this whole business. Still, that's for me to concern myself with. Before we deal with the practicalities of your resigning, have you got anything to say?'

Pearson had moved past the stunned phase a few minutes earlier as the realisation that his career had just ended. The encounters both on active service and in counter surveillance, linked with the mere fact of living in a service sector, all of which he loved with a passion had just been taken from him. With some justification, yet with fleeting intensity, he felt a deep resentment to Jacks and the whole industry of guilt by association he had created. The simple child like gesture of not being woken and told when he had made the decision to leave in order to live a scene from some B movie, where he is unable to talk his friend out the act of heroism or stupidity. Or to say that the order was flawed and that he was fearful. The not knowing equated with being unable to influence and that meant something. As for Chisholm, his virtuous stance had about it flawed nobility, egg shell thin in substance or depth and they both knew it. The noble warrior fighting the corner of an ignoble one had a hollow ring to it. Besides, quite why Chisholm felt any sense of loyalty to Pearson merely added to the perceptible insincerity. And if he wasn't to sign, Colchester, a Courts Martial and more grief without the financial package? Who would care?

Pearson never felt more alone or vulnerable. Even if he was allowed, he couldn't think of anyone able to help or offer advice. His immediate peers or colleagues would only look inwardly at their own careers. To help a 'wrong-un' was not the most shrewd addition to a personal portfolio upon which the next promotion was built. In that moment of recognition he knew he had to sign. He chose his next few sentences with a mixture of care, allied with chance. No number's this time but words from a different place. He stared at Miss Peel, embarrassed for her and her lack or moral conviction. Her neck had not changed colour.

'I don't believe a word of what you said Mr Chisholm. You, along with just about everyone else I've encountered during this situation have not been straight and I cannot abide that. And yet we both know I have no power in this transaction. So before I sign I want all what you have said repeated in front of a third party who in turn will witness the whole process. Your gimmickry and threats do not fool me and as with the last refuge of a scoundrel, had you shed a tear, the melodrama would have been complete. What you have to accept is that one day, you might be sat here. I have no axe to grind with anyone, having done a whole range of things on behalf of the armed forces and her Majesty, only for it to end in a grubby room with me signing away my commission. You had better hope that the person who deals with you were the scenario to emerge, has greater courage than you have shown. As for me not pursuing this, you posed the wrong question. I'm not interested in a claim for wrongful dismissal as I'm not being dismissed am I? I'm resigning, aren't I? How can you object to something latter that you agreed to in all good faith now, is beyond both of us it would seem. So don't link your childish threats to such a flimsy premise. After-all, I shall present a very public face of being content. But I will tell you this and my wisdom such as it is, is based my observations of people, often like you. And it goes something like this. People cannot keep secrets. It is beyond them. Someone, somewhere always reveals a component of information which in isolation is meaningless. But it will add to a tapestry somewhere and so it represents a brush stroke on a wider canvas. Once it is added, the picture becomes more complete but never finished. Secrets, especially those which corrupt or are just plain unfair, eat away at people to the point that they become indiscretions utter by a fool in a pub somewhere or on a bus or to some personal biographer. And yet as with all secrets, it is the story that it shields. Like all stories they have an ending otherwise they aren't one. So no matter what you think you know Mr Chisholm, no matter what brushstroke you are with -holding or the sentence which makes the story complete, there is always another person who knows more than you. And it is they who always talk, always say too much, always premise each little piece of the tale with 'this must not go any further'. But it does. It always does. I can tell by how you are looking that I have struck a cord with you Mr Chisholm and suddenly it is you who looks more troubled. I just hope you know how this story is going to end because there are forces at work here which are way out of your league. So take it from me, I won't have to pursue the truth about Corporal Jacks. Someday, the story will emerge, it maybe sooner than you think who can tell. I really hope you are around to sip from cup of honesty when that day comes because you have shown precious little depth of integrity to-date. People always talk Mr Chisholm. Perhaps now is the time to go and fetch a witness to my signatories and thereafter, you can do me the honor of getting me to Aldergrove and I will leave this part of world for a while at least.'

Within the hour, Pearson was airborne en-route to Heathrow and his mother's house.

*

'And did you fight on?'

Ruth remained beguiled by the tale and not for the first time sensed that at some point she would be compromised hence the questioning about the trust.

'Of course. I wrote to various officials, my MP, a journalist and even some old friends but nothing came back. The only glimmer I got was from a former member of the base who had actually become terminally ill, wrote to me saying that she wanted to die knowing whether it was true that Jacks was a spy and did I know anything more. I wrote back, but the letter was returned given she had died. It was significant in the sense that at least he had been acknowledged within the base but it was very thin. I turned a blank at every call, every letter, everything. I even wrote to the President of Sinn Fein who response was very polite but no less informative. I gave up about seven years ago when I last visited his mother who asked me to stop. She too was dying and wanted to believe that he was a hero for something and if she found out he was a spy, her soul would not rest. Coming from a passionate old lady, blind and virtually deaf, needed to be respected. I told her everything when she asked as she quickly worked out the Army had lied about his death. And now this. Out of thin air comes a glimpse from a man who knows so much more.' He paused and looked at Ruth. He stared at her intently and decided not to reveal the added component; at least not at this point. Before he spoke again she asked him if he intended trying to get more information and could she help-'all hush- hush of course'. His eyes said all what was necessary, conveying the unspoken sentiment which, if spoken would have reflected a sentiment of being unfair to her; something he had no wish to convey or impose.

Chapter 13

The curious smell of warm radiators and hot chocolate mixed with that of carbolic, mop buckets and men impacted the moment he entered the main body of the prison. His morning round was an unusual mixture, that included a compliment from an aged lifer about the provision of daily newspapers. He asked if there was a form he could fill in to denote his pleasure and gratitude. Pearson indicated that he was unsure if any such thing existed, suggesting that the idea of the prison service receiving anything remotely looking or sounding like praise was so unlikely. He remained preoccupied with the events of the last few days. The level of intrusive thought, about O'Dell, a fleeting but significant visit completed that morning, about Ruth and the total absence of the guilt he assumed his emerging relationship would cause him, generated an air of languid indifference which in turn created a sense of calm for others who approached him. His eventual return to his office and the ritual pushing of papers was served to distract him for a further hour when the eventual knock on the door came from his newly acquired friend. Ruth sat down, looking unhappy, almost furtive, affecting an image of someone not wanting to stay. By way of contrast, Pearson looked and felt calm and simply pleased to see her. They looked at each other and with the mutual smiles eventually developing, it allowed for an exchange that progressed things further. Ruth expressed disappointment that he was to be going home tomorrow and that she would miss him, for the few days he was off. Pearson said likewise, allowing them to regress about Twenty years and so experience that curious sensation that equates to feeling wanted by someone else. Acknowledgements were bypassed that both felt OK and clearly they needed to respect each other's professional space. Work to be done and all that.

As the functional office doubled as the confessional, the time felt right for the additional piece of information to be shared. It was to be provided with some well intentioned caveats that the trust that was theirs should not be broken. The demands that were placed by Pearson were done so with such a high degree of intensity that even if you wanted to breach the confidence, you immediately felt that a sign would appear, illustrating that it was you, the person, for whom the cockerel crowed. The demand was presented with a date stamp that required approval.

'He's to be moved later today. I called in to see him briefly as he had already receive a provisional notice yesterday evening. He was so shocked. All teed up now. I got the notification and order first thing. I asked him if he was prepared to say anything more and all he did was to refer me to his letter.' The slightest movement of his eyes was seized upon by Ruth who sensed that this was an important if unclear reference to information that was to add to the picture, awaiting whoever it was to be that was to add to the canvas.

'What letter?' she asked casually but being anything but.

'When we talked last night, I made no reference to a letter he passed me as I left the room. It was unseen by Jacob and it wasn't terribly long.'

'What has length to do with anything? What did it say?' She sensed the next few sentences might prove pivotal to this unfolding, tortuous story. Pearson hesitated but didn't actually look at her until he had finished.

'I didn't say anything because I'm going to keep the letter and react to it. We both know this contradicts the rules and I don't want to compromise you. If I tell you the contents then you are hooked in I'm afraid and that is a career threatening decision.'

'I can always deny or lie of course.'

'You haven't that sought of face I'm afraid. I have.' A smile past between them. They held hands for a moment, so clearing the ground, the space, between them.

'Either way, you won't be implicated. He's given me a name of a priest to speak to, in Ireland, back near Newry. He has suggested that he knows the full story. Everything. If I mention his name, pass a codeword to him, he will agree to meet me and explain what happened. It's a thank you, for me for helping him. The letter says he knew something of me and it was a total coincidence that we met in the circumstances we did. If the meeting with the priest lays a few ghosts, so be it.' The smile passed and a benign, passive look of bewilderment took hold of Ruth; an intuitive reaction, perhaps but she conveyed a sense of unease.

'Aren't you suspicious or leaving yourself open to, well, just about anything? And besides, even if you find this priest and he tells you everything about what happened, what can you do. If this place finds out there is a connection between you and O'Dell and it leads to 'stuff', you will be slaughtered. It is very risky. Well, isn't it? I'm just so very concerned that this whole business is so potentially damaging but ultimately pointless. You can't actually influence anything. Letters being passed to you by an IRA man, reformed or otherwise, is nightmarish if the whole thing...well... what if it goes funny?'

Ruth had become oddly garrulous, agitated almost to the point of indicating anxiety. Pearson was beyond her, and beyond advice. His receptors had shut down. The pursuit of certainty was everything now. Cogs were moving, having been freed by mere chance. He could find out and lay ghosts. His guilt, his pervading sense of guilt would be lifted. Years of feeling outside, not belonging, smeared with darkness and uncertainty. Hour's of no sleep. It will now go away. It will lift, be exorcised and discarded. He also knew that his words were not being heard.

'You are right of course and maybe I'm wrong to tell you. But sat here as I am, it sounds almost corny or trivial to talk about the importance or the effect this whole thing has had on me. Out of thin air, I've been given a chance to find out what happened and to lay down my soul I suppose, to feel complete, irrespective of what I am told. I guess I cannot convey to you or anyone, the burden I've carried over the years and the sense of rage and injustice about my treatment. Being made, forced to end my career with the Army, being ostracised or blanked by old colleagues, all for reasons which are unjust. How can I not pursue this? This issue is about me. It defines and governs my personality such is its enormity. A few words with a priest can hardly do me any lasting damage can it?'

He neither implored nor sought an answer. All Ruth could visualise was the matter not being resolved or concluded. Words would never be able to form the basis of the conclusion or resolution. Absolution was being looked for and it didn't exist. Pragmatically, she could see problems with his job and possibly for hers also, especially if O'Dell let go of his sense of piousness and silence. This whole thing did not feel good.

'I don't think you should make the connection. That's all. You asked for my view and that is it. I for one am not going to doubt your suffering. You are right of course to say it governs you, provides you with a definition. I've never encountered injustice of that sought ever. But this can go horribly wrong.

Look at O'Dell's history. You of all people cannot surely invest your total trust in him, can you? It might be a whole load of complete tosh and then what are you left with?'

A glance at her watch cause Ruth to stop mid-sentence. Standing up she enquired if he intended going home tonight and he confirmed that he was. She asked that he ring her later so as to advise what he was doing. She asked him, quietly, showing a genuine level of concern, to be careful. She then left his office. Pearson again felt absent and detached from his surroundings, wanting only to talk more to his new found bringer of news. He acknowledged his level of arousal, bringing back dormant feelings of excitement and interest. Fear, caution, a sense of balance and an agreement with Ruth about the risks were set aside. This was important. One further read of the letter would help generate a sense of calm perhaps. Clutching at the small, already crumpled A5 sheet, the spider like text said enough.

'I owe you no loyalty or wish to create any sense of expectation or demand. The Irishman within me simply wants to meet a favour with another. After all, what else can I offer? I know you have tried your best to help me? If I do see my daughter but am kept over there, I will, I'm sure be dealt with so what is the benefit of some of my history going with me. None.

Contact a priest called McVeigh in Dundalk. He's based at St.Joseph's-where else! And so long as you go about approaching him in the right way he will help. Mention me and you mention a codename-'Horseman'- he will get the drift. He's a little man with a big heart and is trustworthy but you need to work at his speed. He will know all there is to know about your former colleague, far more than I. There are risks however, which you must recognise and only you can make those judgements. I'm a yesterday's man, a man bereft of purpose or dignity and of no consequence. But you helped me with an unconditional act of good nature. I cannot believe it that I am being allowed to see my daughter and I have you to thank, which I do sincerely. It is strange is it not how principles and values can become unimportant when we want something enough? I hope our respective journeys yield positive results, even if our motives are different. Perhaps they are the same. Ending something is as important as starting, don't you think.

With every good wish…'

This being this seventh or eighth time he read the note, as one might read a card from an old friend, or an unexpected love, he concluded that prudently, it should be destroyed. He would do this later, on his way to lunch perhaps. Or would he do it now? Maybe keep it. Little else was important. He desperately wanted his shift to end, to make tracks home; to a wife he would lie to or at least only tell some of the truth. A strange premise for any relationship to start, with Ruth that is. She knew many truths, his wife knowing few. Best that way, safer. Or was it? He knew that the self doubt would enter his thinking the moment he got home, given the loyalty he felt. Loyalty, matched with a love that sat somewhere between the unspoken and the denied. If it were, he could justify any action in its cause. Loyalty was different. It demanded simple clarity, an unburdening of an explanation for a given course of action. It is rooted within the sentimental virtue of respect, unlike love, with its passion and irrational basis. It also needs to take account of the practical. Bills to pay. Responsibilities to meet. A modest lifestyle to maintain. These elements would pass into oblivion were he to countenance further the notion of seeing this through. Of course, he had every intention of pursuing this but none of getting found out. He had quickly dismissed that this was hardly the stuff of hoaxes and was unlikely to be a fraud, or a trick. The fleeting glimpse that O'Dell had offered, of maybe actually seeing Jacks even though already dead required no further analysis, not until the small priest had been found.

The chance to drive home came upon him slightly quicker than he anticipated. His desk clearance and hand over to an on-coming colleague was dealt with at an unexpected level of speed. He had agreed to talk briefly with Ruth in the car park, wanting to say more than the time allowed and so ending up saying very little. Questions about Ruth's partner were dismissed with an air of irritation, as if that was trivial business compared to events of the previous hour or so.

'You cannot, shouldn't pursue this. You do know that don't you. As your friend, mate, even, the whole thing is just so rushed, so fragile that it just doesn't hang together. I mean, how this man can be trusted. The Priest I mean. In the wider scheme of things, you are something of a nobody who can be put up as the history man, the stooge, the amateur plod, sniffing around for details of an event a million years ago which even if the information you are given is kosher, you can't do much with. I'm really not sure you sense the significance of what you are seeking. If word gets back, you will be investigated and pedalled. At best stuck on the landings at Wandsworth if you come out of it.'

With a flash of a smile that would bring daylight to the deepest moral issue she alluded to the fact that she was hoping to have a different type of relationship with him in the future.

'To allow ourselves small moments of pleasure, outside of the routines that will inevitably continue. Our time. Special.'

Pearson looked at her, changing his posture to present as an attentive colleague rather than a languid equal, noticing two officers with dogs about to pass.

'No matter how much time I take to explain to you the importance this event had on me, I will never convey the true depth of my inner rage, the injustice and the personalised arrogance directed at me when I was still a young man. I cannot stand here and say with total conviction that I was actually close or even shared any sense of intimacy with the guy who died. But what happened was totally wrong and to potentially help myself resolve the thing, might actually make me feel better about myself and improve the contribution I can make. Did you know that my card is marked even within this service? I was told when I passed the first G. board that I would never be allowed to work beyond my current grade. The reason? It was brought to the selection board's attention that they had learnt that the basis of my military discharge was "not all what it seemed". This thing haunts and defines me. I have every intention of going to Ireland but I'll clear the ground first.'

'You are a principled fool.'

'Better than just being a fool.'

'And what if it goes wrong?'

'I'll get shafted of course. I won't mention you if that what you mean.'

'Don't be smart, not with me. That's not what I meant. If it goes wrong over there, what will you do?'

'Survive, I hope.' The flippancy wasn't argued with or challenged further. Ruth walked away in order to avoid any additional comments that had detracted from their time previously. She did not want to engage in a conversation that would alter her view of Pearson, or dilute the evident concern he felt, to right wrongs.Yet her resentment at not being heard appeared to amalgamate with related feelings she was trying to shelve in respect of her now absent partner. He too never really listened. As she walked back to main body of the prison, a tension appeared from nowhere that caused her to stop and pose herself the simple question that perhaps she didn't deserve to be thought of or considered, irrespective of the reasons. This odd sensation caused her more concern than not saying goodbye.

*

Pearson hated driving. He loathed the routine and the fact he couldn't simply read at the same time. He endured the radio, with its sense of wise counsel and learned opinion on all things. His choice of music was often melancholic, creating the need to be reflective and rooted in the past. Driving caused him to daydream, to think constantly about how things might have been different. The reoccurring theme was his own total belief that he was never quite enough for anyone or anything. His failing were accommodated, so often the case for essentially confident beings. His resignation, or resigned state as he once described himself, added to the melancholy rather than cause it. His own sense of self parody and inner scrutiny had allowed himself to carry on. He would always be thinking whilst driving that he wished he could dress differently. Or speak a different language. Others knew more about wine, something he envied. But his constant feeling of being incomplete had, at its root, a truism which was; he was unhappy, incomplete and permanently scarred by events of now, so long ago. He had never told anyone, not even his wife of many years that he met with a counsellor for many months after his discharge. He would often think of her. Her kind features, receptive face and relentless concentration on him, not the issues being discussed. He genuinely felt that it was her who helped him balance and reconcile the anger against the belief that one day; fate would help define some answers. How right she was. Being wise was such a virtue. It was also the masculine element to driving that he found dull. He harboured no desire to be defined by the car he drove but he understood why others felt it important. It was the cliché that was resented, not the belief. Two hours gone, another to follow and so felt he deserved some refreshment. He was tempted by some real coffee at the small but welcoming little road side cafe but was disappointed the moment he tasted it. Tepid, lacking in real moisture and far too weak. It was busy, full of an unscheduled coach party, whose leader was making a fuss about the smoking area. Pearson moved and sat opposite a couple, in their early thirties, deep in thought and argument about what he kept referring too as arrangements. His voice was uncomfortably loud as he persisted in answering his presumed wife a whole series of questions to which she had either no answer or managed to contrive one. She had a heavy cold, looked preoccupied and a little resigned.

'It's a surprise, I'm telling you.' He sounded more cordial now. He then switched into his inquisitor role.

'Did you send Harry to Miss Sue with his jumper and blanket?'

'No. Because I didn't know we were going away.'

'Your Dad will know what to do.'

'When he's coming down.'

'Later today. He's picking him up from play-school. I hope he doesn't forget. Be typical of him if he did.'

'I hope you have arranged him properly- should we ring him, now.'

'Stop panicking it will be fine. Did you ring the bank?

'No. I was planning to do it later but as I'm here it hasn't occurred to me.'

'It will wait. Have you..'

'Will you stop asking me what I have or havnt done when you have done all this? I gave up mind reading weeks ago.'

He squeezed out under the table and walk to the bathroom. She smile urbanely at Pearson who pretending to read an awful tabloid but was intrigued by the lack of synergy in their conversation. Her phone rang and was answered with a snapped formality. It was a friend so she immediately appeared to soften.

'We are staying over for the night, Cotswolds somewhere but he won't tell me. It's our anniversary. He's organised Harry, came to the office and bundled me into the car. The worry is he's packed my overnight things.' The paused response to a ribald comment was greeted with an ironic comment about a fat chance of 'that' given how she felt.

'You can? Great. I'm about to organise some others. I'll let you know how it goes. Or not as the case may be.' The phone call was ended as her husband returned.

'Who was that?'

'Emma.' He was disinterested in the reply and the subsequent series of questions and statements reflected this, looking everywhere except at the person to whom he was speaking. Pearson found his restlessness intrusive. Eventuality they appeared to connect again on a subject about which they shared a common interest.

'Emma and David can make next Saturday. Ericka and her new bloke can't. Your Peter and Jess can do it as can my Peter and his Charlotte so we have a berth to fill.' A series of names past through each of them, with the strengths and weaknesses of each pairing neatly dissected and then wrapped. A newly formed gay couple at her workplace were discounted with the zeal of a middle-eastern cleric, with the nastiness being turned up a notch. A whispered, snarled 'no chance' denoting the lack of breath and so subtracting from an already charmless image. A city type no doubt, lacking in soul but earning great sums of cash. Pearson had, by now given up any further hope of drinking a coffee that gave credence to the name. Allied with a sandwich that defied belief in its lack of taste, he made to move, gathering up his jacket and the remnants of the paper when two more names were presented that made him pause and delay his anticipated departure.

'Ruth's lovely but he really is a complete turd burger. "Liberal in the classic tradition". No chance.

The next facet of the conversation quickly dissolved any unlikely connection between his Ruth and the total unlikelihood of her being a friend of this un-loveable pair sat in front of him. What struck Pearson was how the simple mention of her name had caused him to react. He smiled a short grimace to her as he left the table and did what so many Englishmen do- apologise for moving even though he was hardly disturbing a scene of tranquillity. He hoped their stay in an overpriced poorly maintained hotel in a sand stone village that presented affluence and being forensically clean but lacked passion, was enjoyable. He evidently was doing what he felt to be a good thing. She looked to the entire world as being unconvinced.

He continued with his drive and couldn't rid the image of the aggressive banker from his thoughts. The process of connecting people with their value began in an irritating way, for Pearson at least. What did he expect? Most men didn't like themselves let alone others so why get surprised when such values get espoused in the relative public domain of a road side café. The child Harry would no doubt cope and be loved even so. He started to imagine him and Ruth at their own dinner parties. He would cook. Insist upon it. They would build a new circle of friends, discrete and possibly even of themselves, in a new relationship. Conversation would be optimistic, forward looking, incomplete and questioning. It would be topical, funny, and reflective but rooted in the present. These thoughts immediately made him feel guilty because the opposite was true of his current socialising, such as it was. Social gatherings were undemanding, linear and dull. Discussion was rooted in the past, about others, talked of in the third person. It was too much about schools, house prices, and holidays and, spare him, the weather, and not climatic change. His sense of interest of building a new relationship placed the obvious sexual tension fairly low down the pecking order of importance. Within a few further minutes he had regained his sense of perspective. Spending an evening and some additional chaste moments hardly constituted a life changing experience and the small matter of actually being married helped the equilibrium to settle.

O'Dell appeared from somewhere. The unkempt image of the squat Irishman moved around his head and strangely for Pearson, he could re-create the smell that he generated each time he left the room. Slowly, an uncertainty began to form that was more consistent with the enormity of what had occurred, more aligned or in keeping with the absurdity of what was being presented. Pearson had brought the notion that O'Dell was a man of the truth but even if he were to be asked, he couldn't explain why. And what of the sheer coincidence, the un-likeliness of the chance meeting? Did O'dell really have a view, a perspective on Jacks disappearance? He would have known something, simply by being part of that world. But why the inference that all was not right with the killing of an otherwise unremarkable chronology of events? Soldier falls into enemy hands and gets killed. Neither original nor overly important in the broader scheme. But this was Jacks, who was part of his incompleteness, the source of a series of events that have created more hurt for him than he would dare admit. The self doubt and sense of uncertainty had cause Pearson to drive even more slowly than was his usual norm. The greater the intensity of thought, becoming more intrusive by the hour, the less pressure applied by the right foot. And what of McVeigh? How realistic was it that by such a simple process of asking around, he would find it within himself to tell all. The relationship between the principles of the catholic faith, its church and those who administer the teachings bore only a passing resemblance to what was deemed to be the norm in Dundalk. Often, the priests were the conduit through which 'activity' would pass and somehow receive approval. The term mover and shakers was not out of place when applied to the often small men, all of whom had the personal hygiene habits of an adolescent and would affect an image of being permanently soiled. No one appeared to notice or care, so long as the rituals were followed. Perhaps McVeigh would be different. He would, perhaps, have a slate that was clean, or to be cleaned, a card that was not marked. He would protect virtue and scold hypocrisy. He would be the one who breaches the sanctity of the confessional and tell the police all what everyone knew what was to be wrong. Yet the realism of this was also put to one side.

The truth was somewhere to be found but as he approached his home, the mere reference now seemed to pose different questions. He knew that he had better work out what to say. It would require courage and nerve of course but his compliant wife would say very little, or so he thought. He needed to explain if for no other reason than to outline the potential, small as it was that if his employer made any of the connections that linked him to O'Dell, for whatever reason, the curtain would fall on an already limited career but one which did pay bills. She deserved to know the options but also to be resigned to the fact that he would go to Ireland regardless of the risks and the apparent selfishness of it all. His motives would be viewed as indulgent, the actions of an angst ridden student looking to reconcile truth with perception but having the conviction of neither. He would be viewed by others, if they knew, as driven for no apparent end. So what if he gets told a version of the truth. His Army career would stay rooted along with the undistinguished, the cowards, the white poppy wearers, with the term NTBT (not to be trusted) stamped with the invisible ink which, if heated in the confines of male banter, will burn like a branding fork. The issue of the need for the pursuit will become a feature of the dialogue with his wife. Why wouldn't it when she too has much to lose. She was cautious by instinct as well as nature and was proud with their modest achievements. Consequently, Pearson organised his thinking with equal care and would tell her almost immediately. His overwhelming feeling of taking on the danger transcended the otherwise rational but unfulfilling ingredient which talked to him. This voice spoke quietly of the need to place instinct to one side and balance the proximities that were present and so vital. It could be a complete con, a lie, a perverse trick played by O'Dell who knew some names and took pleasure in creating the dance. It could be a last hurrah, a set up, an attempt to take from Pearson his history or to parade in front of him some memories. It could be a faked rationale for creating the conditions in which Pearson was to be tested and then to be found wanting. 'So he would follow a lead given by a prisoner. We thought he might be suspect and so now the proof.' All implausible but each element found a place within the voice. The dismissal, however, was swift and without malice. He had every intention of going despite, despite what? Despite everything.

His house was 'executive' in design on a small village based estate but actually lacked a decent room. It wasn't quite the 'top dollar' the selling agent had promised but it was pleasant if undemonstrative. Like thousands of similar houses all over the country, it being neutral had an appeal. He was met by his wife with an unconditional, broad smile, the one she would routinely summon on his return. They had met after he had left the Army, but just before he put pen to paper to join the Prison Service. Small, pretty, uncomplicated, reserved, occasionally dependent and totally without, what his mother would have called 'side', she quickly became part of him. She once disclosed in an unguarded moment that her abiding emotion for him wasn't that of love. It was the fact he made her feel safe. Consequently, the relationship developed around an unspoken understanding that great passion would remain absent from what they did and very early on, a quietness descended on their mutual baring, where the swings of intensity which characterised other people's relationships were not present. During dark periods, in which he would dwell in a melancholic haze, Pearson raged at himself for not having greater capacity to share, to give, and to be also dependent on someone. But it wasn't to be. Consequently, the relationship developed an ordered sense of balance, punctuated with occasional highlights of humour but not fun, intimacy but not the love that others share. The birth of their daughter provided the glue that held both the physical as well as the emotional bond to account. She was enjoyed with a zest and an intrigue that had no limits. Consequently, that relationship now conducted from afar was as close as anything Pearson had experienced.

"Never have any secrets and you won't go far wrong", was one of those truisms his mother would utter but the older he became the more he knew he found this stance pointless. From day one, he decided to tell his young wife- they moved from the point of contact to the alter within Twelve weeks for reasons which neither could explain- very little about that period of a few years in service. He found talking about it almost painful, frustratingly unable to communicate the pressures he had experienced and the intensity of the fear he had encountered. He viewed that he would become the bore, a caricature of someone who claims to have been someone but in reality was one of many. He also felt that it was strange how a few years experience when young could then shape the remainder of his adult existence to the detriment of everything else. When at dinner with friends or questioned by people met on holiday, references to a hidden past were pushed deftly away and supplanted by time spent 'in insurance' or travelling. His wife played along, not wishing to create any additional unease and showing loyalty that he felt he neither deserved nor warranted. He once overheard her talking to friend, comparing his attitude to the past to that of a small boy suppressing a poor school report. The task of hiding the content became more important than the content itself. He found this an elegant analogy and as can often happen, liked the feeling of being surprised by these remarks. In many other ways, their lives were manageably separate, neatly facilitated by Pearson's reluctance to move for the sake of his job and choosing to live 'off site'. Healthier and they both believed that it was right for their daughter: an achiever at school, popular with countless friends and rooted to the insular world of the small village. The tempo which his job had created allowed for a verbal freshness to be sustained although it took away from other components of a relationship that never really fully achieved a foundation or an emotional base upon which to build. Strangely, they behaved in each other's company the same way now as some many years before. The lack of intimacy was demonstrated through an ease of dialogue that one might identify with close colleagues. The highs and lows merged into a sameness from which Pearson in particular took no comfort.

Routine questions, about the journey, about the car, about work, moved around some general statements about their daughter's plans for the weekend, the house insurance and other items of domesticity. It also included reference to his wife's mother visiting tomorrow; maybe they could go somewhere. The mother in law cliché did not form part of his views. She was a delightful individual, funny, intuitively sensitive and shrewd. He agreed, suggesting the coast perhaps or even the shops. He had no preference. He alluded to a possible need to go away for a few days and take a day or so for leave, if that was ok. Their absence wasn't so sustained that his wife didn't pick up the voice emphasis that conveyed doubt and uncertainty.

'Go where? Not more training surely.' She looked vulnerable, and quite suddenly concerned. When asked to, she sat down and was attentive, intensely so, normally as one might have associated with a doctor or a priest. The irony of which appeared not to be lost, initially by Pearson and later by his wife. He commenced, having first set the scene of this being a difficult time and somewhat pathetic reference to a closing phase in his life that would help both of them, a statement he immediately retracted. He was aching to leave his own skin, standing in front of his once love, looking devious and uncertain. The time was now. He drew the words from deep within, alongside a reticence that was clawing back each syllable as they wove a thread of coherence. He was hating this, a scene, choreographed but ill-defined. A prompt, a quip, allowed him to at least start.

'We haven't really ever talked of my time in the Army for reasons I've never fully understood. That says more about me than you I think. But something happened which for whatever reason has caused me pain and some anger ever since.' His wife made an insensitive remark about this being a magazine moment when you tell me you are gay. A look and the necessary half smile reduced the comment even further.

'Having been posted to a specialist communication centre in Northern Ireland, I was a section head of a watch who filtered intelligence reports. Much of the work was routine and straightforward but the whole place had an intensity about it which defied belief. No one was allowed out of the place which was a condition of the posting. My watch handler was a guy called Jacks, a really good man from the Black Country. We spent hours with each other with the usual division between officers and ranks going by the board, talking, playing chess and so on. One morning there was a gathering of all the senior commanders in order to plan for a special operation. The following day, Jacks had disappeared; the first time ever a person had left the base without permission. An almighty row blew up with all kinds of claims being made. I was placed under special measures, and withdrawn from operational duty- the guilt by association thing. The next day, Jacks body had been found, having been shot, executed, presumed by a paramilitary group. I was arrested, questioned for what seemed like days and then dismissed from my commission. I was never charged or brought before a court martial but was simply got rid of. I wasn't allowed to speak to my commanding officer because the whole station thought I was somehow implicated. My grieving for Jacks has never ended because it was never allowed to start but I hope you get a sense of the strength of feeling I have needed to retain given the dishonour, the lies and the actual feeling of not being able to at least influence some thinking about me. It has been truly dreadful and I suppose has been reflected in the way I am or act. Ever since those times, I have been seeking a truth, a certainty about why this has happened to me and also, what did actually happen to Jacks. To this day I still don't know.'

He paused and looked fleetingly at his wife who was transfixed and engaged in what he saying. Her feelings were taking her onto the ending of this story because she had never heard him speak so fluidly or with such sentiment. It was this that worried her most, rather than the content. She had always assumed that something unpleasant had happened about which he did not wish to speak-not uncommon for a soldier.

'Almost unbelievably, I think I have met someone who knows something about what happened. He's a prisoner who I have helped to visit his sick child and almost as a thank you, has alluded to thing with Jacks and has passed me a name of a priest in Dundalk, Ireland. Mention the prisoners name and he will help, that kind of thing. It's full of risks, it's irregular, very irregular but I almost feel I don't have a choice. I'll be dumped if work make's the connection but I want to go and if it comes to nothing, I've lost nothing. Equally I might find a version of the truth I can live with.'

He was sitting forward in his chair, personifying the unease he felt, even as he spoke. His conviction however never wavered and his wife quietly absorbed the details of what he was suggesting. The lounge in which they both sat retained an air of not being occupied. The carpet remained pristine and even the suite, purchased a decade earlier had some plastic cellophane wrapped around one its legs, having survived a three time per week vacuum. Everything was in order, clean and just so. The atmosphere that was evident reflected this. His wife, the uncomplicated Linda, was visibly churning over the connected and unconnected points. The gaps, the linkages, the related doubts, the misunderstood motives and sense of feeling so driven all worked on her. She wasn't able to look at him, preferring to hide her uncertainty by looking out onto a garden, dominated by lawn with little colour or having a sense of being imaginative. Her silence dominated. She resisted any quick or cheap analysis of the issues being presented preferring to settle on an initial view that was so typical of her; one which put her husband's needs first irrespective of what she felt. For the first time since they had met, however, she didn't fully trust his motives but concluded that for now that would remain unsaid.

'I suppose that if you think it might help you then you should go. As you said it is fraught with risks but if you are convinced that the end justifies the means. And if you don't go, your demons will remain with you I suppose.' Her delivery was calm.

Pearson expected a different response from her but one no less thoughtful. His guilt was tempered by the irrational dominance of what was right for him rather than her. As he made to move she spoke further, in the manner of a panellist on some phone in and retaining an objectivity that he felt he never deserved.

'You have obviously thought carefully about the consequences if it goes wrong although I do wonder of you have seriously extended this to either Jenny or I. I also assumed that you have pieced together why a prisoner would presume to have generated sufficient intimacy with you to the point of telling you something so profound. After all, you were only helping him in accordance with what is require of you. As for contacting the priest, you have no doubt given some thought to being led something of a merry dance and he might simply lie. Equally, it might be some elaborate set up to settle some unspoken old scores. So, if you go and you are satisfied with the outcome then so be it. But you may find that in fact more questions are left unanswered. That is the risk it seems to me. And remember, your happiness is relative to mine.'

The poise of her comments left Pearson feeling less assured. They were all valid and thoughtful and as she continued, the axis of power and control began to shift.

'Perhaps it is also worth asking the 'why now' question?'

His response, crass and un-thinking was so typical of his benign indifference.

'That is because I've never met anyone since now who had ever said anything about it?'

'I didn't mean him. I meant me. Why chose now to tell me of your past. You have barely ever said a word about it since we first met. So why now? Why confide in me, now?' The question reverberated around and around, given its direct fairness. Fairness and persistence were unpleasant bed fellows when being their unwelcome focus.

'When individuals chose such a moment, having overridden countless others, it would suggest they have made a conscious decision to do so. Such a thought process would suggest an element of hidden guilt perhaps? You haven't got much form for spontaneity. So, why now, why tell me this now? '

She continued to look deeply beyond the line of elms which divided their patch from the field beyond, full of grass ready for silage in some six weeks. He wouldn't answer the truth that dare not speak. Guilt did play its part, posing questions of the human spirit that ordinarily remains hidden. He conjured up an unconvincing, lame response, muttering about the time felt right and neither of them could dismiss what this prisoner had said. She retorted that he could have done, dismissed it as some fantasy land guess work or a stunt.

'But how would he know?'

'Well you've got me there because I didn't so perhaps the intimacy shared with this man suggest greater knowledge than even your wife could muster.'

A bitterness had now surfaced, rarely heard during so many years of unspoken resentment of the lack of simple talking. Etched into her tenses, like shards of glass, they scraped unexpected parts of bare skin or in this instance, emotions.

An evening meal was shared punctuated with the audible movement of cutlery and the deafening movement of glasses, unbroken. A short conversation came and went about their daughter. Self contained and organised, the natural parental concerns which seemed to follow young college students were less evident with each of them. She was a bright, able girl who set her own parameters and placed few demands. A third party diversion would have proved beneficial for each of them at this time as the afternoons conversation moved around the room but never settled. The cutlery appeared to be getting louder when banal comments about contents insurance, the window cleaner and the vet. Pearson caught a reflection of themselves as the dining room door caught a draft and opened, revealing a half buried hallway mirror. He looked stooped, unhappy and distracted, his wife managed to hide the fleshiness of a pretty face by allowing her hair to look disorganised and worn long and with it a simmering resentment about his lack of faith. Often a home coming would follow a similar ritual; of chores, fluid conversation, a meal with friends concluded with the shared but awkward intimacy which irregular lovemaking often produced. This was not to be, today. A dull film was half negotiated followed by going to bed at separate intervals, so creating no expectation of touch or the simple act of holding. Pearson's mood had grown darker, having two elements to consider when he wanted only one to be present. He remained seriously perplexed by his wife's reaction, as though it was planned, rehearsed even. This didn't make it any easier to mitigate or to make the decision to go.

He woke at 3am and knew immediately that he had little further enthusiasm for more sleep. He went to the kitchen and within seconds had drunk Two pints of milk. He then sat, trying to absorb how he was feeling. Ruth came and went quicker than he imagined and hoped she was missing him. This thinking bordered on the self indulgent which wasn't helpful, preferring to try and locate his feeling about going to Ireland and to pursue Father McVeigh. But they wouldn't come. His wife's earlier views simply reverberated around and around, like all the best moral questions. He made an attempt to answer her question that concentrated on the "why now", as it was the fairest. He reminded himself of his reasoning that allowed the comfort of the personal to override what others needed to know. His wife was no different he felt but clearly she thought otherwise. Why wouldn't she. What was it about people who wanted to hear of other peoples secrets? Even if they were enquired after by your wife? It didn't naturally follow that the past needed to be shared, not to Pearson at least. On this occasion, however, it seemed to.

More checking was needed, he concluded. His wife's references to motive of a self redeemed maker of terror merited further analysis. The discordant harmony of a man offering up a favour in return for an act of compassion did not neatly fit. Pearson's act was one of unconditional professionalism. O'Dell's retort was deferential, dependent even. Do this for me and I will give you a treat, sir. Strangely, the requirement to root out truth had taken second place to his own motivation of testing O'Dell. Perhaps this would pass. He found mornings quite cluttered with a range of tasks, rituals and routines that needed to be negotiated before the day begun. Being at home, 'off', was no different but for the time being, the distraction was welcomed and relished.

Linda fussed and rattled, putting away, picking things up, and washing plates with imaginary crumbs. Cupboard's appeared to lose their silence as they closed. Her body shape was one of; you have started something but expect nothing in return. She left the house at the speed associated with resentment but not indifference, leaving him with more time to think. Who could he phone to discuss this matter with? Which friend could be depended upon to share thoughts and concerns, to listen but not preached. Advice was needed not correction. No one sprang to mind. Ruth perhaps but no. He would ring the Prison in Ireland on a pretext, to engage and quiz O'Dell further. Foolishness of course. He would correspond, write anonymously, seeking more information, reassurance, certainty. More foolishness. He would approach the Regiments chaplains to help, broker a deal of some description. Quickly dismissed as fantasy. Balance had given way to the pursuit of something more; even though it was unlikely it existed. Was Jack's really that important. Dead for well over a decade and still no external word so why was it important. This type of internal questioning barely required a reply, no matter how quiet. To not know something as large and dark as this grated and scraped, a stone in the shoe culminating in the mind being unable to settle. But what of the answer? What would he do with the knowledge? Who would be told and at what price? And still it churned around. He would write to his MP, table a parliamentary question on his behalf. What would it consist of? The enquiry concluded that Jacks left the facility without permission was captured, interrogated and duly shot. No longer news, one of several to meet such a fate although often without such evident disquiet. What would McVeigh say? What significant piece of information, or detail would he hold to lift the cloud? Or perhaps create an even darker aspect. Doubt and a prevailing uncertainty was taking hold. Gradually, the squeeze felt harsher. The intrusiveness of these thoughts was beginning to worry Pearson.

His torpor hadn't noticed his wife's return and the cooking of lunch. They spoke further. However reconciled or otherwise their being together, it required a response. That would include him trying to speak with McViegh, if he could be located and if required he would visit. The consequences, considerable in terms of his employment and the certainty of his mind, were balanced against the relenting need to know something. Employment loss was a much greater consideration. Again the mood darkened with Linda, by now, having returned with no fuss but evidently seething and tearful, frustrated with her own lack of influence. The speed of it all, how things had shifted from manageable co-existence to that of chaos, uncertainty and likely grief. Still she could not reconcile the imperative of one person's wishes against her own. Within a few minutes, she quickly concluded that her view, her opinion, her ideas, however presented had no worth. She had no worth. She was trying not to beg, or hector, or sound anything other than right. But the words did not flow, they couldn't connect with the person she hardly new or recognized. What is it about a few sentences amidst the multitude spoken over the course of years that creates the shift? She knew they would never recover from this. It was that deep. This was being unfaithful to her sense of self worth, worse than a relationship with another- this being tangible, something to push against. Years of no reference then an announcement. Why tell me, she thought. The hurt was such that she felt sick, light headed, and unable to concentrate. She would talk with someone, her Doctor, her friend Dorothy, measured and understated someone to give the alternative perspective. She understood men better than her; she felt, knew how they ticked. Had a violent husband and three sons and so on. Pearson suggested that this wasn't wise- telling others created what the security world used to call 'ripple'. 'I'll be the judge of that' spat Linda. The more who knew, the greater likelihood of not achieving the desired effect he suggested, a point that wasn't appreciated or understood by either of them within moments of it being said. He tried, without success, to see her point of view, to stand in her space and look through her eyes. But he couldn't. Her concerns were dusted aside, realigned as one might an arm chair. They had no value, or resonance. They counted for nothing, and she knew it. The space between them had again moved. It was apparent whatever their relationship stood for, it was built on sand that once was fresh and light but now had shifted. They were standing on nothing. Nothing. But he would go. He must. He stated one further time that for him, he must seek out whatever truth there was to hear.

Chapter 14

Leave was approved unusually quickly. The yarn about the chance for some Golf in Ireland appealed to others. He allowed himself three days to at least established contact with McViegh, to confirm his existence if nothing else. He knew that it wouldn't be difficult, establishing his presence that is, but creating the climate to talk would be fraught with complexity. Hopefully O'Dell had at least conveyed some sort of message but who was to say. The anxiety about any risk had passed unlike the words with Linda. They had ended once she drew the line in the absent sand. 'It hadn't even occurred to you that I might have wanted to come, irrespective of what I said. You are a cruel person' she claimed. He was uncertain what to take, or how to look, concluding that it best be casual. How odd he felt travelling by car to ferry without a tie. No logic of course. Round and round it went. Could I be damaged by this, could this hurt others? What if McViegh lied or shouted April fool, like he had hoped before, in a different place. He had no reference point to locate what he felt. Maybe that didn't matter. Determination in the pursuit of truth was noble. It was the truth he was seeking, helping to provide some resolution to his growing concern about the crossing. He never travelled well on boats but maybe today would be an exception. He never quite believed that the car would still be there after the churning across what were only a few hours. A meal, a newspaper and short sleep, avoidance of any talking to anyone. He made some notes about the type of questions he might ask were McVeigh to appear. How to get to the facts without seeming vulgar or indecent. He knew he must avoid developing his censorious tone-how could priests involve themselves in matters of crime rather than sin. Was McVeigh present when Jacks died? Did he administer the rites to help appease others in that 'I'm above all this' fashion. Being their to prevent or intervene might have been more godly. But conclusions should not be jumped to. The power sat elsewhere and not with Pearson. Best not condemn and sanctify just yet.

The drive North from Dublin commenced, he immediately started the dwelling, the re-playing of old mental tapes. In silence. Still the nerves failed to tingle which felt strangely unnatural although his thoughts moved to and from Jacks, his family and the unimagined terror of his last few hours. Subservience, that construct humans encrust from the formative years always sat uneasily with Pearson, despite his natural, foreboding allure. Time spent in his company was rarely wasted or forgotten but his personal puzzlement was how it was sustained. Especially with a person like Jacks, whose personal authority and dominant intelligence was equal if not stronger than Pearson's. The reoccurring image of tea, cakes and the like being served from a tray was playing like a visual loop one might see at an airport. To go beyond the security perimeter and not risk being either spotted or identified was so odds on, so limited and consequential that he started to resurrect his previously held explanatory thesis: that Jacks was ordered.

The terror, the undiluted terror or being compelled to leave the base and do something, having not set foot outside for months remained incongruous, of course, although every argument put forward was quietly broken down by his inquisitors. The hypothesis was tested, relentlessly as Pearson's position was dismantled. The Command gives an order to a Junior NCO to leave the base without transport, for him to do what? To move in area in which he had no knowledge or transport. He had no specialist training and his instincts were counter to those used by Special Forces, or even a mere fox... And to do what? To deliver a birthday card or some groceries? To assassinate the Queen or meet with collaborators or the enemy or no one or everyone? What did he stand to gain? What was his motive or the special information he had that made it so compelling that he should be allowed to leave. That he was so special and different and unique that he and only he could break the convention? This analysis was time and again ridiculed by his minders with the counter argument deconstructed like lead, melting in a furnace. That Jacks would obey an order to leave if issued but he was neither especially brave, practical nor resourceful. If anything, his clumsy nature – 'mother said I was dispracsic but as we couldn't spell it, we didn't let on', he quipped- would put him at the back of the queue for any being asked to do anything furtive or require guile, speed of foot or even being brave. His strengths were thinking logical, not acting illogically. And even if ordered to do so, he would have told Pearson, conveyed a message somehow. Other details resurfaced. Did they remove his glasses before placing hood or tying the hands? He lied about his eyesight consistently; avoiding tests and re-tests skill-fully. But they were poor. This feature of his execution always upset Pearson; it being somehow even more inhuman to shoot a man in the head not just blindfolded, but almost blind. The perversity of the human condition such as it was. He opined to his handlers that if he was ordered he would have tried to have left a message for Pearson, coded and encrypted. That much he accepted. When asked how he could talk with such certainty about a junior rank, Pearson's response sounded feeble and thin, mumbling something about 'feelings', tacit reaction and so on. The handlers dismissed this as the language of inner guilt which surfaces when a belief system has been eroded. Jacks was a human being with his own needs and wants. Having pursued these, he was shot, so say the handlers. That you never really knew him counted for little or merely compounded the belief system that sat within the gene which control's self determination, personal greed or chance. He was pre-programmed. Jack's acted out his wish. It would be foolish to deduce anything else from his behaviour. So stop it. Why bestow yourself the honour of being the special one, the recipient of the explanations of why people behave in systematically corrupting ways. You can't because they can and do.

And yet the doubt persisted, remaining as strong now as ever. Pearson rehearsed his lines again. He must control any rage he felt should he meet with McVeigh. He, like others, would have being doing his job by being the custodian of secrets. That is what priests, after all, do. The shield, the screen, put blankets over unwanted sights or words, their motivation or purpose unlikely to be questioned. This is what they do. They were part of kaleidoscope of ever changing colours or rules by which they were sanctioned. It had little to do with God but more to do with a much more higher power driven by status. To be part of it made people feel alive and priests, for all their suppressed grief and denial can't resist being chosen, not by god but by the local commander. The provision of sanctification by a person who did not pull triggers but through the manipulation of hand would affectively say it's OK, its God's work, so making whatever was necessary OK too. The corruption of the thinking, the thin hypocrisy created the anger within Pearson, not any sense of action. Just don't call it Gods will. A similar argument with Undertaker's would be had, at another time. Having located St. Joseph's he reckoned it would take him twenty or so minutes to walk. He would catch the early evening mass and wondered if he would blend in. He didn't care. He wanted to get on with it, whatever it was.

The arrival at the gothic, tardy looking edifice took a little longer, having stopped to buy a newspaper and a more detailed road map of the outlying district. He looked at the latter to see what he could discern from the years that had passed. What was immediately apparent was that the centre from whence Jacks departed was nearer the border than he recalled. This wasn't felt to be of great significance but it jogged a memory that might need to be revisited. From nowhere, tension started to take hold. His left hand started to shake and he was unclear if he needed to sit down. He perspired to the point feeling as though it would become aromatically noticeable if he actually got inside the church. A few moments of standing still, quietly, pretending to read helped the desire to turn round pass. He was very alone and he knew it.

Ireland and this part of it were hostile to the point of strangulation. It looks English of course, with every aspect, every inflection of the architecture representative of Victorian Britain. But it was neither Victorian, British nor Northern European; that was a mere disguise. It was a facade of resentment dressed up to mask a deep seated hatred. And Pearson was in its midst. He looked and walked differently to everyone else, probably smelt differently too. The cloying nature of his anxiety wasn't passing as moments of fear came back from his nightly patrols, the car boot, and once getting isolated from his men when they were charged by some young people, launching petrol bombs. He tripped over, became concussed and as the blows rained down, a batten round managed to disturb his wide eyed assailant, all of 13 years old.

50 seconds more perhaps, and he would have gone. Never had good balance, he thought.

He regulated his breathing and began to settle. He chewed some gum, and started again to walk nearer the church. It was not the grey sprawling mass that transfixed him, simply the rather unkempt display board of emerald green and peeling gold leaf. Third name down, complete with the academic notation's illustrating his Doctor of Divinity. Father James McVeigh, Priest of the Parish and so on, one of five celibates officiating beneath Father Patrick Felish- a name he never knew existed. O'Dell was right about one thing, so far. He glanced further at the board and noticed that Mass was later than published which explained the absence of the usual precession, often of older folks with grandchildren. The church was open and with some 40 minutes to lose, he went in, ignoring the parish notices and the published list of up-coming confirmations. Various Saints also needed to be celebrated and thanked at various times during the week. He hoped they would forgive him if he over-looked their needs for the time being. He located a pew that he gambled wouldn't belong to a family or some oligarch; anonymously placing himself behind the eighteenth century pillar and aside a newly constructed plinth. He sat, feeling very self aware but noticing, like a creeping early evening tide, the pews placed within several feet of the altar began to fill, as anticipated, with the shuffling elderly and the younger more boisterous children. A nun caught his eye and she stepped forward to pass on the order of service, the prayers to read and the mass to be celebrated. She said nothing and he assumed likewise. He was trying hard not to think that everyone was looking at him, wondering, jumping to conclusions, and putting the word out. He knew this unlikely but he also will anticipate that someone somewhere will enquire, ' first time?' and with it the rituals with which judgements and the coded analysis, that sit beneath the questions, would cipher the response. Times had changed even in this provincial town but not to the extent that a stranger would not be noticed amidst a hundred or so regulars. A mixture of isolates, groups, pairings and a blind person being lead were now moving purposely into place. He noticed the tolling bells for the first time, always evocative, calling out the reminders. The congregation stood as the celibates moved serenely down the aisle, uttering the callings, swinging the incense, causing several of the younger people to fake their coughing, and furtively giggling. Large men with white tunics, woven with the tapestries and insignia of their orders and as always, their rank. The status of each priest skilfully denoted by their positioning at the altar. He stared intently to determine who might be McVeigh amidst the group. The age of one priest enabled him to be immediately eliminated. The others all looked like similar, of an age, with a look, thin, caustic, and forbidding. The greeting was made and effortlessly the gathering sat and was invited to prayer. Pearson hadn't witnessed this scene for over 20 years but he was able to pick out the tempo, the order of things. The level of attention and participation was beyond intense. He had forgotten what it was about a gathering that bonded people, concluding it wasn't the spiritual but the routine. An hour of certainty, when others took on the burden of the day. Tension really was left at the door, he could tell.

Within a few minutes his speculation about who might be McVeigh ended as he stepped forward, having first been invited by the lead priest, to offer the psalm prior to the communion. There he was, the oldest of the group, the most frail and faltering until he spoke. His voice belied his frame; strong, concise, authoritative and direct. He quoted the gospel according to Paul and used the allegory to make contemporary references to the local world. The need to give, to share, to look after others, to shelter the poor. He pressed home the point about duty. God's work. Amen. Pearson couldn't help his internal speculation. Duty, caring for others, balancing the spoken word with actual deeds. Quite what McVeigh really knew about the past bared little scrutiny? He too must have his share of burdens. Being a priest hardly disqualified him from dealing with his own demons, irrespective of what his own vows allowed. Secrets, confessions, more secrets, more confessions. He would be expected to deal with them all. Condemn less, understand, rationalize more, and explain away acts that would make Saint Paul weep. McVeigh needed to be the circus act, the high-wire expert, the clown and the ring master, coordinator of the illusion played out in public but no doubt resented in deep recesses of his private thoughts. Already, Pearson was making judgments about the old man, giving him the benefit of the doubt before anything had become between them.

Bread was taken and wine supped. Thanks were given. More prayers were offered and no doubt taken as the order of the ritual was gently worked through. The tranquillity was momentarily broken when a young child caught her finger on her mother's coat and was twisted accidently to the point where tears and scream came but quickly passed, amidst much reassurance and head stroking. Noise in a church remains as incongruent as snow in summer-they do not belong, shouldn't happen. The concluding psalm, sung with dignified beauty by the small choir, the colour of the sound which did not match their individual presentation. Yet their sound resonated and echoed around the steep walls and beyond. It was a moment of calm during a process where he never left his seat, declining the communion or the kneeling during the moments, described by a previous Army Chaplain, as shouting demands silently to God. As the Mass concluded and the procession left, espousing the Latin of Benedict, Pearson was thinking quickly about how to make the first engagement, the first connection. How would they both engaged when they looked at each other. Who would take the initial lead, to develop the first signs of the presumed intimacy that was needed in which a dialogue could take place? He couldn't work out how the natural order was to unfold, especially as the tide was going out. He was being left as he came in, on his own.

The celibates' were bidding farewell, individually, to each person as they walked from the main entrance, making their way back to their early evening meal. Perspiring heavily again as, he approached the line, he shuffled into place. Even if he wanted to by-pass the reception, he was unable to. Like fluid into a funnel, he found himself squeezed out of the aperture, landing at the feet of the tired, grey collection of authority. Each person was thanked, there hand clasped and suggested that God would be with them. Fourth in line was McVeigh and as the hand was extended, Pearson asked if he could speak with him privately, suggesting that they step aside, away from the last remnants of the gathering. 'Surely', was the quietly spoken response, gesturing that they step back inside out. Both men trod gently and turning on his heal Pearson took the initiative. He had already rehearsed his lines, recalling the notes he had made. Closer up, McVeigh looked even older, displaying a vacant stare from a face devoid of expression or warmth. Dark ringlets sat beneath eyes that had a greenish hew. His face resembled a collapsed rock face with layers of folded skin cascading beneath his cheeks, past his throat and beyond. The richness of his hair was detracted from given the film of dandruff that had settled on his dark suit that sat underneath his robes. He looked for the entire world in need of careful attention, proper food and perhaps the need to bathe. He was the type of priest that would reduce a class of children to silence, their parents to recoil.

Pearson thanked him and made a complimentary remark about the mass, the turn out. He also made the point, obviously but without wanting to sound crass, that he was a visitor, with a purpose and would welcome the chance to explain further the purpose of his presence. McVeigh said nothing but inflected that he could talk openly here, now although it was evident that he was not yet engaged. Pearson began to seek that strange oddness that allows people who know nothing of each other, to talk on an aeroplane, often sharing significant intimate details, then at the point of landing, step away. He hadn't reached this point yet, not even remotely close. He quickly re-played the tape. Eight days ago he knew nothing about O'Dell, McVeigh or their link with his past and here he was talking with the latter on the directions of the former. A colleague ambled over to indicate that the church was to be closed in few minutes. Pearson took a step and mumbled an incoherent sentence stringing the words of long time ago, English, death of a colleague, O'Dell and so forth. Coded references were overlooked. He was apologetic but it was important, he said. He would like the chance to talk further. McVeigh stared at Pearson, his eyes penetrated beyond the beads of sweat that had collected. He looked calm, disinterested and withdrawn, to the point of almost not quite believing what Pearson was requesting. There was no flicker across the face, no movement of the hand, no modulation of the voice. Just an amiable silence. He was not godly or sympathetic, neither concerned nor emotionally aroused. He was present but absent.

'Where are you staying, I assume locally?' Pearson confirmed and explained further about his journey, his timescale. He also iterated that it was important but not urgent. There was an uncertainty about how to acknowledge the inherent risks that were present. It was suggested that they meet here in the morning, around ten, pronounced 'tin' in an accent that was from the deeper south west.

'You will appreciate that I'll need to make a little more sense of what you are requesting and we need more time of course.'

'You know O'Dell?' The questioned wasn't asked are posed. It was phrased as a matter of fact with the chase having been cut to.

He stood and presented, again without engagement or a shrug of compliance, like a man awaiting the arrival of a train.

As they walked slowly to the door, he volunteered little by way of acknowledgement of the name – he neither confirmed nor denied- saying quietly that if it's who he thinks it is then it's the family whose daughter is poorly, and that he minister's the family. He made no reference to O'Dell' the senior. 'Tin O'Clock, then it is'. Their hand shake was passive, lacking the certainty of before and eye contact was not held. With urgency but falling short of desperation, Pearson pressed a little further; seeking reassurance and approval. He wanted recognition of the investment in time, what it had taken to bring him to this place. An acknowledgement that this was no ordinary moment. This was a big, dominant theme, a defining moment for one of them. And for these feelings of turbulence and uncertainty, the lack of caution and the incumbent risks to be viewed for what they are. That McVeigh would keep his word and be present was necessary to be confirmed. That he wouldn't now simply absent himself from what must be tense for him too. He too would retain his own sense of foreboding. The sins of his past might come to rest. The transaction wasn't entirely one way, surely. Questions surfaced quickly. Why did he want time? He knew already how to join up the dots, fill the gaps, and answer the questions. He knew what he knew. Pearson became irritated that more acceptances did not pass. McVeigh said nothing further, but continued walking; leaving Pearson to leave the scene with a sense of inner turbulance that nothing will come of the request. He felt dismissed, pushed to one side, not selected for the team. If he never saw McVeigh again, it represented a chance lost. The irony that this priest could truly pass absolution in a sense that might provide completion, that was real, with permanence, was felt. Or did he get asked this type of request frequently but without ever answering. Questions, but no answers. Answers to the wrong question. Both crashed into each other as the reluctant behaviour of one caused such uncertainty in the other. Nineteen years and the moment was lost. Like being in darkness before the eclipse and remaining there forever. The walk back was ponderous, lacking the optimism of earlier. With no appetite he decided that a drink might assist his sleep. This was after all Ireland.

In the morning, he decided to check out of the hotel, such was his intense discomfort with all elements of the past 24 or so hours. The absence of some fundamentals-sleep, recognition, the given and receiving of hope or optimism-were all missing. The phone call home engaged the answer machine and not much else. He was dwelling to the point of boiling and McVeigh was hardly likely to reduce the flame. The speed of his transportation back to Ireland, physically as well as emotionally to confront something more than a demon had now become diminished. His preparedness for failure exposed limitations that had not until now featured and yet he knew he was exposed.\He anticipated that there would be some local chatter about who or what he represented, caring less about the evident threat but more about feeling foolish. The tread back to the church was consequently slow, laboured and merely ambled without conviction. Pearson felt and no doubt looked foolish, to compound the conclusions already completed. Perhaps he was destined to know nothing of this contorted, abstract puzzle. Other than him and the parents of the executed Jacks, the memory had been reduced to photos and cuttings in the shoe box, set deliberately at the back of the wardrobe. To be produced by Mr Jack's father when seeking sympathy from his visiting carers, whom he bored to the point of anger such was his comic book, B movie plot line ramblings.

The main church door was open, lodged back deliberately. He walked in at the point where footsteps sounded behind him. It was McVeigh, looking more welcoming.

'Oim to have a coffee so I'd say that you'd join me.' A statement, not an invitation thus he followed without hesitation. The church generated the smell of part of his childhood. Of games being played in a sanctified area, enhanced by the ghosts that were watching them. They located a small room, laden with papers and the unfinished cigarettes, unframed photographs, tacked to a grey, concrete wall. Pearson sat, resting his left elbow on the desk, looking at McVeigh as a patient might a Doctor. The coffee was welcomed and fresh, surprising them both. McVeigh never sort his eye but Pearson felt unwilling to talk, he simply sipped. Very English

'It's a business ain't tit'. A mumbled refrain. 'Always some folk wanting to seek out the past no matter for how long gone tis was. Always. But I sense your one of the different kind. The type who seeks truth before he story is finished. We don't meet many of those here, you all know why now of course. Even allowing for the changes, to ask these questions will always cause pain. You will know that right enough of you'll will. Relax a little will yeah, twill allow some breathing to go on. I'll try and help as I can but no promises of course.'

The two men wandered around the story, trying to agree dates and times, the months and so on. McVeigh listen with intent and persisted in his contradictions. Pearson wasn't right, he suggested but with no edge or sense of resentment. He was being, in his own words, 'right'. Pearson listened with almost child-like forbearance and McVeigh weaved a spell but necessarily not one made by any alchemist. The discourse from the priest moves the discussion from the history of the seventeenth century, to migration, to the trenches of the First World War. 'Our people faught alongside yours you know and when they returned home in 1917 were stoned and abused, wus than any German could muster. Crazy times of course and no wonders'.

He asked Pearson why yer man in prison should talk about such things now; why now; why the timing. Did he know why? He came at the issue is various ways and Pearson detected a shift in what passed between them. 'He obviously new a great deal of you, more than your name but it seemed so random simply to talk with you to curry some type of favour. Beyond a redress.'

'I assumed it was just that: an opportunity to put something right. And I achieved the desired outcome-he got what he wanted and if his child benefits then that's good. It must be good. Not all soldiers bare a grudge-from either side'. More gaps within the story were filled but often at the expense of what Pearson felt to be accurate. His probing and further questioning of motive was casually brush aside, leaving him perplexed about the extent to which McVeigh was bothered. At what point should he push home his wish to have his real questioned answered was now about timing. He wondered further if McVeigh was already getting distracted by the risk he was taking in talking. Where was his authority granted, and by whom.

'What does it give you Mr Pearson, once the details are agreed? What will it do to you or perhaps for you? Knowledge is different from understanding. The republican cause then as now was very simple.

You have moved on and closed chapters, no?'

'No, I haven't. I was dishonourably discharged after only 20 months service with no chance to redeem or salvage my reputation. I did not lie about Jack's as others had suggested and yet his motive and reasoning remain both untested and poorly understood. Few people walk to their death willingly. It is a mystery and one that haunts me. I feel I have chance to try and understand what happened and why. I'm repeating myself, I sense.'

Doctor and patient; the former ignoring the latter. McVeigh's mood became more hostile, suggesting that all this wasn't just about Pearson's needs. He invited him to think very carefully about risks and consequences to others including him. That absolution wasn't just something god had invented. Confession was real for the person making and receiving it. Without any sense of reasoning, or context, other than to appease his own discomfort, Pearson suggested that they both could do with a walk around the church grounds, an offer McVeigh rejected. He wanted to ask his own questions before they went any further.

'You are a careful, studious sort Mr Pearson, not someone who will be casual with the language of motive or reason. O'Dell picked his moment didn't he, to create some ripples. So it's not just about you or me. He's in amongst it somewhere too, no? Maybe it was coincidence that he posed you these questions, remembering your legend from a time past. It is very neat to the point of being almost complete. Had he not gone to your jail, the logic is that you and I would never have met up, yes?' Pearson stayed with him for the moment, agreeing the basis of his argument. He quickly concluded that he was unlikely to have known where he had worked but it's not inconceivable. McVeigh offered his version.

'Yer man orchestrated his transfer to your place and place's his demands and it worked like clockwork. Your people, not unreasonably would not have joined up his motive with his game as they did not factor in your element. He got what he wanted, to see his child. But he also had a simple alternative motive; to involve me -the priest from the old days, to embrace me back almost.'

'Embrace you back to what? You are not being overly clear.' Pearson was taken by surprise that his counter-balance had become almost aggressive and sneering almost to the point of confrontation.

'Too fekking right I'm not. With clarity brings insight and we are not ready for that yet'.

Shuffling his papers and placing his coffee cup to the rear of the cabinet. He stood up, announcing that he needed to see a family. They should meet again later, around six maybe a bit earlier if he was done. Maybe a friend of McVeigh's would join them. Pearson was, without any sense of further hostility asked to leave. His legs barely moved such was the extent of the combination of fear, dread, of uncertainty and surprise. The reference to being joined by another was very unsettling. McVeigh throwing a different scent.

Not knowing what to do, Pearson took the decision to enquire if it was OK to sit in the Church. No it wasn't. It needed to be closed. It was suggested that the library should be visited, maybe to look up some old records from the past or to simply sit, a suggestion Pearson decided against sensing now that he was to be followed or watched. He was deeply troubled and resentful towards McVeigh but was unable to explain or express why. He too must have been perplexed by what was happening and perhaps why.

He found a phone box but his calls, to home and to Ruth were unanswered. He left messages, indicating that he would phone another time that he was OK and would hopefully be travelling back tomorrow. A coffee shop thereafter. His stomach felt as though it was clamped, amidst two great forces. Palpitations came and went, matching, probably causing beads of sweat to meander down his back and oddly only on the left side of face. Inevitably he questioned what he was doing, how to balance the quiet hostility from McVeigh against his truth. He dwelt on the obvious, unable to rationalise anything. Nothing went away. And so it churned, round and round. He rehearsed his lines, again. Jack's death was never investigated thoroughly; he knew that from his original contact with the Police. The acute embarrassment that abounded reduced it to a file, unsolved. Part of the missing or the myriad of sectarian killings where the tacit cultural agreements allowed for some, not all, killings to go unchecked. But he was no further on in his understanding of what part McVeigh played. He knew the details but his spitting words directed at O'Dell were not expected. His simplistic view of the brotherhood allowed him to believe that each relationship was balanced and born of tolerance and understanding. He assumed, again simplistically, that O'Dell's motivation was clean, not soiled or tainted or contaminated by a further need to create further pain. Despite his murdering of the law man, O'Dell had never overcome his own sense of guilt caused for his wife and young family. That in itself made him human.

His coffee, untouched and merely pushed around was cold. He forced himself to think of his own home and his daughter. How his darkness meant he was only ever a conditional father; conditional on his mood on a given day or time. His withdrawal into a world of books, of watching sport on TV had diminished himself in his own eyes. Other dad's were better than him. Other husband's were also better, more attentive, interested and part of a partnership and not simply of it. Further he dwelt. His feeble attempts at getting closer to Ruth now seemed child-like, almost approval seeking rather than anything of substance. Earnest discussions about her relationship, moulding itself into their contact and by doing so, giving themselves meaning. Yet it was a fake. McVeigh had caused the reflection and exposed what wasn't real or complete, what was unlikely to be answered. Like an imperceptible film that sat beneath his clothes, he felt not part of anything or anyone. The man serving the hot drinks brought him a fresh one. 'If yer face was the weather, I'd not be putting the washing out'. A raise of his finger acknowledged the easy sentiment of concern. Pearson liked the simplicity of the man's job. You make a drink, a sandwich, you wipe a surface.

The glancing at his watch forced the hands to move. 5.27pm. ten minutes to walk. He couldn't wait anymore. Was this how people felt when getting the result back of tests? The trite comparison irritated him simply as they were pathologically ordained and not without certainty. His walk was to generate feelings more akin to the stride to a border guard, 60 years previous, with a star stitched on to a lapel. Will he allow me to pass or seal my fate in some other way? His stomach felt laden to the point of being unable to stand properly. His collar and his belt were too tight, restricting his movement, or so it seemed. He paid his due and walked out, being startled by the bell on the door as he left. It was raining heavily, discolouring the small terraces all to blood red, glinting with a reflection. The Church appeared and he considered walking around its circumference, to waste or perhaps kill time. The look at his watch confirmed that some ten minutes were needed to occupy, or at least that what he thought. He heard an unexpected call from a small window next to a side door, suggesting he entered. It wasn't the voice of McVeigh but he responded.

'Mr Pearson, you'll be catching your death wandering around. We are to meet just along here. Father McVeigh was just having a quiet moment.' If he was a clergyman, he wasn't dressed as one. His garb was a traditional dark suit with a red fleck in his tie. Younger than McVeigh he guessed, he affected an air of a manager in a men's outfitters, fussy, concerned, interested but time restricted. McVeigh was present but looked vacant and said nothing.

'We've about an hour before evening mass so let's get on with the business. My name is Cornell; I'm a solicitor who represents the diocese and look after the likes of Father McVeigh. He's invited me over to sit through a meeting, a discussion I suppose. He wants' me to take note and to oversee any subsequent course of actions. There's a degree of formality to these things but they ought not deflect us away from the task in hand.' His comments were articulated as he organised the room to accommodate the three, no doubt unwise men. Some paper and a pencil were laid out, neutrally. McVeigh looked even more distracted, unsettled and ill at ease. He momentarily stared at Pearson whilst persisting with the stroking of his Rosary. At no time did Pearson feel compelled to talk, ask a question or do anything other than observe and follow the quiet but busy authority of the shop assistant. With further detachment, the shop assistant set out the position as he saw it.

'Father McVeigh has explained how you come to be here and the sad business of a dead soldier several years since. He's also explained that a Mr O'Dell with whom you have spoken has indicated that Father McVeigh might be able to provide some information about these events. You have established with Father McVeigh that he does indeed know Mr O'Dell, having helped his family in the past in pastoral capacity. You have done the same it seems. What is troubling Father McVeigh who I might add has been quietly impressed with your approach is what in essence do you want? If its information to the point of naming names and the like you will understand that is not likely to happen. Father McVeigh has no knowledge of the person responsible and besides even if he did, he would be forbidden to say; such is the sanctity of how these matters are communicated. The sensitivities associated with these types of meetings, how they are seen or perceived are fraught with difficulties. I'm sure I need not spell out what can and still does happen. These are no longer the 70's but feelings run high'.

His delivery was crisp, his accent mixture of high Celt and English; maybe from Edinburgh. He clasps his hands in front of himself and he looked directly at Pearson. 'Father McVeigh is very anxious to help but would like some assurances about how you might use any information given. It's a question of good faith, respect as well as an understanding of your predicament. Father McVeigh has indicated that this sorry business has troubled you for years; your career and so forth cut short. Your mind poisoned and troubled by the sense of accusation.' Pearson has conceded his authority completely to this diminutive yet forceful person to the point of regression. He wanted him to sort things out and to allow him to leave. But the texture of how the words were moving around linked with what wasn't being said would not result in such an outcome. Pearson spoke.

'The only assurances I can give is that I will respect what is said. To act upon it-go to the police or whatever is neither part of my agenda or theirs. The Military have suppressed this story to the point that they are unlikely to thank me for resurrecting it. It's really is for me and some extent his family. For them to not have any kind of indication about what happened is just wrong. They were treated appallingly. As for me, it's affected my whole being for years-not knowing. O'Dell recreated something of the scent that brought me to here. If the Father is prepared to provide some form of outline, that will suffice. It will stay with me unless of course you choose to tell anyone else. I have no hold or 'sway' over you and your people, do I?' The question was ignored. Cornell flecked, such a movement regenerating uncertainty within him but at least some of the ground had been reclaimed.

'Father McVeigh will say a few things', and he immediately stood up and with his hands deep in his pockets, he peered out of the window for what seemed like an week.. His neck sinews twisted back and forth. He started to talk with a tempo and an, less cordial than before and more measured.

'Jacks was a fool and created a problem that was neither sought or expected. The boys were to start running an insider at your place but were not getting very far. The information they were wanting was never likely to come their way so they were to target someone. You Pearson. Put pressure on people you know your family and so on. They would stop at nothing but they needed an Officer type simply as the range of material he would be exposed to make it more worthwhile. They drifted some material in for you. Carrot and stick. Money or serious damage to your people. Yer know how it works. They sent the material in and waited. Straight forward sit and wait tactic. You were given a window each night to either leave the camp or find a way in which material could be sent out. The boys new your place was totally restricted but worked on the basis that you would give in. They never reckoned on you not seeing or getting the material. That was foolish of course. The types who leave brief cases at bomb scenes. Out of thin air, this soldier appears and presents himself as you. Within a handful of seconds and two questions we knew he was lying. He was questioned further then executed and the whole fishing trip was abandoned. I tried to intervene -the man was simple, a wreck, trying to be someone else for a slice of glory but who knows why. And before you asked, he left the place by cutting a hole in the fence at the rear of the main gate-lodge. The camera was unable to cover that spot. He told me that. He knew he was to die and asked for a final confession but the poor man was so terrified he couldn't say much. He idolised you Pearson, wanted to be you or at least protect your soul. He thought he could carry it off. Pretend he was you, run bogus data and words and become something special. Madness. Utter madness. The deed was done. He was brave but utterly stupid.'

The shop assistant interjected, not really allowing a sense of mood to become too settled. Pearson had quickly absorbed the detail. His immediate instinct was to rebut what seemed an unlikely narrative. His memory of Jacks, did not equate as some kind of pleasing wannabe, as a cloying sycophant, the taker of apples for the teacher. He wasn't mad either, or remotely someone likely to turn or jump ship. His tour was nearly due. By some odd quirk, Pearson had lost his tension and had become more focussed on the story.

'There you have it Mr Pearson. Uncomfortable listening but something to make sense of we hope.'

Time was drifting, as he noticed people gathering in the mid evening greyness outside.

'Not sure whether to laugh or cry such is the enormity of what I've just heard. Forgive me if I neither thank you nor accept the account at face value. Even after so long, it doesn't relate to how I remembered the man. Honest, loyal, uncomplicated and almost devoid of cynicism. He wasn't likely to fall in love with me either- or if he did, personal sacrifice in the face of utter and certain death was a large price to pay.' A glance at his wrist and he stood up adjusting his jacket. 'How would your people know that I was able to receive the information? The random nature in which information was collated could no more guarantee I would receive a message than if you wrote it in melting snow. Why not simply write to my parents-send a card or something.' He knew he was being dismissed, fob off, not being taken on the outing but the elders had neither the courage nor personal sense of duty to explain. This yarn was neither a hint nor even a half truth. He doubted McVeigh knew very much other than O'Dell's name. Even if he was present, he evidently chose not to listen. What could be worse than knowing everything other than the not knowing? He stared at McVeigh, rehearsing the only insult he could drag from his own mortality, suggesting that if this is what faith does to an elderly Priest's sense of decency then the level of hypocrisy was best shared around. The glance from McVeigh said nothing, more than nothing. It confirmed in Pearson he was a fake, an imposter, the man who wears the frock and lights the incense but believes in little else. A fake and one who smelt shamelessly of a cloned cast and his breath having the odour of denial.

'What was sad father is that you had so little influence. The use of priests as a neat signature to allow death to be quietly inflicted was feature of those times I never understood. Having neither the courage to join or oppose just to sit neatly on some holy cloud and dispense whatever was needed.' He looked at Cornell.

'I'll honour our agreement but you will understand that I might need to talk with you both maybe later in the year. Not now. We three know your explanation lacked decency or logic. By all means treat me as an enemy but I'm not foolish or without empathy that the questions I posed were difficult. But your response was that of people who offer only an image of your Church. O'Dell suggested you could help. Maybe even he might be disappointed in how you have treated me.' Cornell coloured but McVeigh allowed his face to absorb Pearson's sentiments. His soul was shut down. He shuffled out, his legs moving again, the blood finding his feet although his heart needed more. The walk back to the hotel was denoted by a lengthening stride and the churning of the detail. Material intercepted. How did they know about me anyway and for him to assume an identity of an officer and simply cut open a fence to keep a speculative assignation was indeed madness, and unlikely.

His appetite for more had faded during the length of time it took to locate his vehicle. More questions, with sustained sadness. And to think he couldn't find a sort was absolution in a Church of all places. Having decided to take the earliest ferry he remembered nothing of the crossing or the late drive back. 6.15am the next morning he arrived home and what he noticed immediately was the gap in the drive and the curtains opened.

Chapter 15

Three days away and his return acted as a metaphor. The house, clean to the point that it would defeat a forensic scientist seeking evidence that people actually co-existed. Everything where it should be, not matched by who should be where. A cursory note was left on the notice board asking that the papers be paid for. Had it said paid for and cancelled, that was likely to be more accurate as that was more of a reflection on what was evident. He had been cancelled, a sensation that was easily felt when it was present. He phoned the control room to determine who was on duty, hoping it was Ruth but it wasn't. She along with other managers were not yet in - a note saying she was due in at 10am.He felt he wasn't where he should be so, having climbed the stairs, he stood in his daughter's room. It reflected her mother, not him. Ordered, perfumed but not warm. Ordered in a way that was opposite to how young people should live.

Through the process of his shower, he decided that he would go to work. It was apparent he had nothing else to do, a further indictment of the fact he could find the energy and a focus to travel and search but not relax under his own terms.

Too early to call his wife's mother-the likely sanctuary where to deposit herself and her feelings and unwise to call Ruth, he was left to drive some more. He dwelt on the shop keeper- he must remember to check his registration with the law Society - and his approach; cursory and without sin or motive. Round and round and round again. The story remained incomplete and not one he was likely to share with Jacks parents. The wannabe hero who stopped a bullet for the boss he loved. The incongruity of it spelt out further uncertainty complete with gaps and omissions. And maybe he was wrong to go. He felt worse now than before if that was possible. He regretted not asking further questions about what he disclosed when being tortured. He hoped he spilt all the beans to spare himself unnecessary pain. Who produced the pillow case- starch white? An item of utility to ward off night time dribbles and stains, to be washed weekly for years and stored. But not this one-its pair was left abandoned someplace. This one was destined not to provide comfort but merely to shield his eyes from those about to empty a nine millimetre shell into his head. The dribbles caught were entangled with tears and blurts for mercy; spittle and bile and vomit projected the seconds before the stench of carbine. Breathing restricted and with each last few gasps, the cloth entering his mouth and retracting like a skin of a snare drum. It caught and absorbed the blood, also. Someone would have produced the small piece of bedding, had it to hand and it struck Pearson that of course it was someone's job to get a pillowcase, have it ready for its unintended use. He should have probed McVeigh further. He had already grown to dislike him and his hypocrisy- his dancing on a pin approach to morality. To be present when a man is executed and rationalise his subsequent inactivity or unwillingness to mediate and continue to pray: characteristics that struck Pearson as both thin and cowardly. The church of Rome, with its rituals of excess and preparedness to turn the other cheek was present of course when Jack's was killed thus making them guilty for sure. The shambling, unkempt, odorous McVeigh and his failure to influence modelled so much of where and how his Church and others could affect their own escape from their own prison and prism. Perhaps when he gave him his living last rites and absolutions, he offered God's forgiveness. 'The afterlife would be better'. Then the click.

He concluded he had achieved very little. That McVeigh and Cornell had lied, perhaps or maybe were content to issue their versions of their truth. He would contact O'Dell, set out what had been said. He would breach his agreement to 'respect' the confidences of others. He would spell out to O'Dell the story and await the reaction. Was there anything else he could do? He also sensed that this, his Gestalt, was dull, uninteresting to others. He would explain to Ruth his motive an put it to bed. His wife too would be brought into his world. He would try and lift the mood, lighten the darkness. To be more present, more interesting, not joyless and changeable. He would focus on his career. Try harder. Take the next step. Remove his label as being awkward. Contribute more. Be political. Attend conferences. Write some papers. Study further. He would change. He had been given his own absolution, a version of history that was partial but at least it was a part of something.

More driving and although uneventful, the twist in his stomach was more developed. The gate lodge was empty save for the officers issuing keys. They appeared tense; the lack of the usual jokes and irreverence was marked. His tally when placed into the shoot was met not with the clunk of his keys, but an envelope and a simple refrain.

'I'm to escort you sir, as instructed'.

The note was barely readable but clear enough. 'To report to the G1 when on site.' The uneasy sense of going through doors, having to wait and the dance that arose when straddle between an air lock. He could make little sense of what was happening. The carpeted area of the Governors ante room was to be the end of a long walk and one not wishing to be repeated. The officers knock was met with quiet greeting. Lionel looked calm, his desk less than the immaculate paperless receptacle it usually reflected. Pearson was invited to sit but evidently not talk. Lionel had perfected the school master's art of creating the suspense without the rage but the atmosphere appeared less humid, more devoid of sentiment or aggression. Lionel moved from his desk and sat opposite his almost but not quite and simply stared at him.

'Forgive the melodrama of the keys. Needs must.' This simple turn of phrase neatly organised his thoughts, placed into a hierarchy of likelihoods and grief.

'This business with O'Dell, this visit to Ireland and the manner in which you have gone about things. Not good. Created considerable noise upstairs, most of it has reflected on me of course. There is to be an investigation. Gardening leave until the matters done but anything less than blood will not do. Whatever your motives, your reasoning or your simple intention, your conduct was ill considered, potentially dangerous and almost certainly embarrassing- for the Minister and I'm on his side. You are viewed as an indulgent arrogant fool. You should have talked to me before anyone else.' He deduced that Ruth had briefed, confirmed within the next sentence.

'Ruth, amidst tears and no little anger, told me the whole story. She was right to do so.'

Pearson was already ahead in the next round of conversation. He regressed, switching back to being talked to by a different man at an alternative time. So he asked if he could explain what he had done, and importantly, why. Lionel listen with care and sensitivity, observing the pain of his almost friend as he made no attempt to justify his conduct. He simply wanted to provide the context. Passive indifference was the dominant ambiance but at least he felt listened to.

'I have known you for a while and you have carried something during that period that has been evident in all what you do. The albatross not only following the ship but steering it. Or should that be driving? On the merest of a whim, offered by a serving terrorist- no doubt calm and responsive as they often are-you go off searching and enquiring of matters unlikely to ever be solved. And yet you brief no one other than a junior colleague. It looks not only ill considered but an act of desperation: a great puzzle in which the final piece has now been found. Or so it seems. I know it goes deeper than that and our judgements often get muddled when the pursuit of certainty offers us something more. But you have acted without intelligence or foresight. This is the confusing bit more than the act itself. And I suspect your underlying question has yet to be answered. Often the way. Amidst all of this - you are likely to be sacked and remembered less for high principle and guts but that you did a turn for a man who kills Judges. People rarely understand motive but will recall and scrutinise the net impact of the behaviour of others through their own eyes and rarely do less than condemn. Your burden and your pursuing might define you but it will be of no interest or value to others. It will seem indulgent and dull and disloyal, not selfless or noble. That is why it looks so bad-looks being everything. Within a handful of days, your judgement is shredded. You have turned inward on yourself for your own ends and by not embracing the views of others or advice, you create the impression of arrogance and disloyalty and yet I know neither element to be true. Ruth's anger was more about the consequential impact on others, including prisoners that your absence will cause than directed at you. The words she used about you reduced your motives to a wanting to self destruct- a kind of self fulfilling prophecy, now fully achieved'.

Pearson had no quarrel with the man sat in front of him. His offer to resign was rejected for beauracratic reasons rather than those of morality or a wider principle. Allowing the investigation to run its course up to the point of outcome could take months. At least he would be paid.

'Enough now of the self flageration. Go home, make the piece with your good lady and rather than look inward, look outward. The chap who died; you will never ever know what his real motive was-that word again-and judging by what you said, the person who shot him in the perfunctorory way terrorists have when doing such things would have rationalised their behaviour out of the window. It was business. There motive would have been to complete a day's work so to speak'. Secrets, secrets, secrets. Some simply have to remain just that.

Officially you are not meant to call me but ignore that callous rule. I'll keep you posted about this end but it really isn't looking very good. Blood on the carpet and all that.'

Leaving the Prison and the slow amble to his car, he was approached by an officer, keen to explain himself; an issue of lateness and so on. Pearson smiled and advised dialogue with his manager. Motive.

He drove to the flat to clear a few things. Four phone messages, numbers noted, were again wiped unheard, even though three were from Ruth. He had no appetite to hear her condemnations or otherwise. She too had her motives and in this instance they were protectionist. Consideration for him, however undeserved was evidently just that. And how would he respond; as a colleague or friend or potential lover? All seemed unaligned and misshapen in how the relationship was to be conducted. If any such relationship existed. In this sense, he felt foolish and small, marginal to events rather than of them. His next mistake was to sit down, then back. The reflection, the dwelling on half-understood references began to churn and move around. Anxiety surfaced then retreated, Certainty gave way to more questioning and then back again. From nowhere, seemingly, the tears rolled. And rolled. He shook violently, convulsing into morass of saline and congealed mucus, weeping like a child would after being found out. Except these tears were invisible. He had no one and to complete whatever process he had started, he concluded that perhaps he never could. He awoke some three hours later, cold and shaking. He had slept in a ball and had held himself so tightly he has left indents on his ribs. He was completely crushed, broken in half and exposed. He had no capacity to do anything other than dream. He closed his eyes as before, wishing beyond hope that they would never again re-open, not until his dream had fixed things.

About the Author

This is Michael's first novel and draws on elements of his own experiences and those of others. His own background is rooted within the Criminal Justice System having worked in and managed custodial servies and support for the victims of crime. Currently, Michael balances his professional life as an independent consultant and policy advisor with a desire to write. He is currently preparing a screen-play based on this, his first published work. Living in Cheltenham, Michael has three daughters and a grandson, Oliver.

Printed in the United Kingdom
by Lightning Source UK Ltd.
132611UK00001B/4/P

9 781434 392336